Sea of Silver

Osmarie Pico

Preface

One morning, I was bored at work and I asked myself what I would do if money were not an issue. What if I were not stuck in the four corners of my workstation? The first thing that came to my mind was to write a book. I started to google how to write a book, and from my research, I developed a theme, a main character, and a plot. I do not know what happened to me, but once I developed the theme, I felt that a creative spirit possessed my soul and drove me to fulfill my childhood dream to write a book. I finished the first version of this book in four weekends, basically eight days. After I finished the book, it sat on my laptop for a few years until my professional mentor, who also wrote a book, told me he published his book because he wanted to share it with the public, not to just keep it on his laptop. That was my wake-up call to share this book with the public. I began by sharing it with friends for feedback. My first reader told me I should write a series because she had questions, and she wanted a continuation. It was my intent to create an ending that left something to the reader's imagination. Her feedback alone gave me the inspiration to push my book into publishing.

This book is a product of my imagination, but I incorporated my experience and the collective experiences of people I have met. I rose from poverty, but I am a dreamer and a believer in myself. I was born and raised in the Philippines, later lived and worked in the U.S. for a year, and I now live in France. I wrote this book to inspire my reader to go beyond borders, to take risks, to challenge norms and standards, and most importantly to follow their hearts. I added the love story because I know everybody loves to read a love story.

This book is dedicated to all women, to those individuals born to a single parent, and to anybody who believes in dreams and is passionate enough to uncover life's mystery. I want to give hope to everybody so that each reader understands and follows the flow of the universe and dance with it because I believe that we all have a purpose in life. It is up to us to discover it.

Sea of Silver

CONTENTS

1 THE ROUGH CHILDHOOD

It was 7 o'clock in the morning and Elena's first-class would start at 7:30. She still had a four-kilometer walk to school, and her mother was nowhere to be found. Elena thought of lunch. She needed her allowance before leaving for school, or she would go hungry. She contemplated her options. Either wait a couple of minutes longer for her mother or leave and pray for good luck. She waited.

7:20 brought Elena a miracle. Her mother arrived and handed her a twenty-peso bill. She quickly explained that she had borrowed the bill from the neighbor. Elena looked at the bill, disappointment written all over her face. It was not enough. This was not the first time her mother struggled to get money for food, and Elena couldn't help acknowledging their misfortune. It had to be tough being a single mother in a small village in the north of the Philippines. Elena's alcoholic father left them when she was four years old, and she could barely remember him. All that was left in her memories were of the fighting, shouting, and her father beating her mother. Her mother was determined to lift them out of poverty by making ends meet, from cleaning houses, doing neighbors' laundry or reselling some vegetables and meat. She had seen how her mother struggled to get them through each day. Her mother exerted an enormous amount of effort to send her to school and to hand over today's allowance. Complaining was the last thing she would do. Elena held back her tears, forced a nice smile, and bid her mother goodbye.

She had a tough day ahead of her but as usual, she would let her lazy classmates copy her assignment. The small fee she would collect would help her get through the day with enough money to buy decent food.

She arrived in the classroom late, catching her breath as she rushed to her seat. Elena listened to the shuffling of papers as her classmates handed in an assignment. She quickly realized their teacher had just given a surprise quiz. The best of her misfortune today.
In the past few weeks, this had become a normal scenario for 12-year-old Elena.

"Of all the times to give a quiz, why did it have to be today?" Elena murmured under her breath.

She had a long day at school and a long walk home. Elena's dark brown skin blazed under the scorching heat and the intense humidity matted her frizzy hair. She was hungry, but thoughts of finishing her homework and helping her mother with household work made her numb. At a young age, playing had become an illusion and working had become a ritual.

It was going to be a tough night. Poverty was a curse that she didn't have the option to reject. The dream for a decent meal during lunch breaks, new clothes occasionally, and an end to perpetual poverty pushed her to work harder towards success.

She walked on the road with tricycles and jeepneys passing by. After walking for almost an hour, she reached a small nipa hut situated beside a small vacant lot attached to a big wall, the wall of their rich neighbor. She reached home. She opened the fragile door made of bamboo and the sight of their humble abode greeted her. Their house had a small table with two long benches from each side, the living, dining, and kitchen all together in one small area. There was a bedroom with bamboo bed where she and her mother slept. There were two small bamboo chairs beside the dining table where she put her bag. Elena sat on the other small chair and pondered over how she could get out of the situation. *I need to get a scholarship in one of the greatest schools. I don't think it would be that hard. I just need time to focus and study. I need to make sure they like me during the initial assessment.* Then she daydreamed and planned everything that seemed just beyond her reality.

"Elena," her mother's voice interrupted her daydream as she opened the door

"Yes, Mom. I just arrived, and I have some homework to do."

"You can do that later," her mother said. "Help me with the laundry. I have three loads of laundry that I received from three different customers. We need to finish it tonight so I can hang and fold them tomorrow."

Elena walked towards the stack of laundry with great determination to finish it early so she could finish her homework.

While washing the laundry she continued dreaming. She imagined herself with celebrity white skin and silky hair. *I will have the money to get that white skin when I grow up.* She thought. *I will also have the money to buy those nice clothes and not just wear these same old clothes every day. Ah, it would be great if I became successful.* She imagined she had become rich and famous, traveling the world, and eating in fancy restaurants with a prince, like those in telenovelas. She imagined living her lavish lifestyle and coming back to show her classmates that she had made it. They would all envy her success. She was tired and hungry, but her thoughts made her smile. Elena remained in the wonderland in her head dreaming while her small hands washed the dirty clothes.

"Stop daydreaming and hurry up. It's almost 8 o'clock and we still have half to finish. I will leave you to prepare our dinner, and I will come back to help you finish," her mother shouted.

She didn't understand why her mother prevented her from dreaming. "I like to dream, I like to imagine, I like to visualize and I like to feel that one day these things that I imagined will become reality," she hissed as she continued washing the laundry. If she didn't become successful, she would end up like this – washing clothes every day. She would live the same life as everybody else in this village. She wanted to get out of the village and see the other things that life had to offer.

"I will become successful," Elena said as she scrubbed the laundry. "I will do whatever it takes to get out of this poverty."

Her dream was something that fueled her to become successful in life. She collected old newspapers, magazines, and books from their neighbors who wanted to throw them out so she could sell them on the open market for money, but she gained more than just money for food. Before selling them, she would read articles about successful people and businesses and imagine a different life.

Instead of filling her head with ideas from newspapers and magazines, her mother constantly pushed her to excel in class, but not for the main purpose of having a bright future. She wanted to brag to the neighbors' children. Elena didn't understand this concept because she believed excellence should be an expression of passion and interest rather than for the purpose of bragging. The constant comparison and bragging were the norm in their village, and this caused jealous thoughts in Elena as she observed material things in her environment. At a young age, her village was her only environment and reference about life.

They finally finished hanging all the laundry at 10 o'clock in the evening. Her mother cooked a humble meal of rice and canned sardines. It was good enough to refuel her drained energy from the day's work. She made time to finish her assignment after washing dishes.

■■

A few months later:

"Good afternoon. It is of great honor and pride to deliver my commencement speech today. I never thought I would finish on top, but I was always determined to deliver excellence in everything I do. I was not wrong because it paid off. This is not a long speech. I will try to keep it short and simple.

I want to share that there are three things that helped me get here today standing in front of you. First, it's all about having a dream. It is no secret to all of you that my mother and I are as poor as dirt. But I am rich in dreams. My dream to get out of poverty is fueling me to push harder in life. Our graduation is just the beginning of what is about to come into our lives. I know that my dreams will direct me to the right path in life, so I will not stop dreaming and yes, I dream big.

Second, perseverance and discipline are the vehicles to achieve the dreams. My life is not easy. I struggle to help my mother make ends meet, but I persevere no matter how hard it is. Sometimes I feel like giving up, but I put discipline in everything I do and that's what makes the difference. The small effort we make every day will at some point make a big difference.

Third, to the parents of this graduating class, support your children with their dreams. If they don't have one, encourage them. We, as your children, are a reflection of your masterwork. If you guide us to the right path and

constantly remind us that everything will be alright, we will believe that everything will be alright. We thank you for giving us the foundation as we start this journey called life. We thank you for your patience and unconditional love and, most importantly, for giving us our daily allowance.
To my mom, thank you for all the sacrifice. I know we will be able to make it someday. To the parents of the graduating class today, congratulations. You just finished the first step. There are other difficult steps ahead. Good luck. To my classmates, we made it. I know we are all looking forward to the school holidays before we start our high school days. Let's enjoy and cherish the moment before we take life seriously. To my teachers, thank you for the knowledge and guidance you have vested in us. Rest assured we will try our best to behave. To all of us, let's celebrate this glorious afternoon with pride. Thank you."

A loud applause filled the small commencement hall as Elena finished her valedictory speech. People were smiling, some had tears in their eyes, some were laughing, but everybody felt proud and happy after Elena's speech.

"Elena, congratulations," her classmate said as she approached. "Where are you going for high school?" Catherine was one of Elena's rich, bratty classmates who rarely ever spoke to Elena.

"I'm going to Holy Trinity Science and Math School."

"Are you kidding? That's an expensive school! Can you afford that?" A doubtful, insulting smile was plastered on her face. "How can your mother afford to send you to an expensive school?"

"Yes, I know we are poor, but one shouldn't be restricted from pursuing her dreams because of the mere absence of money. I tried my luck by applying for scholarships and I was granted free tuition and a monthly allowance throughout my entire high school." Elena was irritated but she answered with humility.

"Oh! What a stroke of luck you have. Well then, congratulations."

"Thanks! By the way, where are you going for high school?" Elena asked.

"San Antonio Public School," her classmate replied.

"Public school? Why? I am pretty sure your family has the money to send you to expensive private school," Elena said.
"Um, I didn't pass the cut-off score for entry in Holy Trinity," her classmate replied.

"Oh well, sorry to hear that. It's hard when you have the money but don't have the brain cells." Elena shrugged. "Money can't buy brain cells."

"Well at least I can afford to buy nice clothes," her classmate replied in an irritated voice.

"Well, good luck with your expensive clothes." Elena walked away, leaving her classmate irritated.

She realized that God gave her intelligence as a gift, and it would be her ticket out of poverty. She was overwhelmed with happiness when she thought of her scholarship and the ability to continue her education. In a poor country like the Philippines, she knew that education was essential to survive the challenges of adult life. The definition of security was getting a good job in a big company.

2 LIVING THE DREAM

When Elena ended her presentation, the spattering of clapping sounded like falling rain. The familiar faces of her colleagues seated at the long, oval table seemed to blur into the white walls of the Manila conference room.

For a moment, she was back in the small village she grew up in, struggling with the heat and humidity in the shack she shared with her mother while a tropical rain drummed on the roof. She was the 12-year-old girl alone and starving, waiting for her mother to bring food home.

Elena sucked the coolness of the air-conditioned room into her lungs and shook her head to clear her thoughts. She forced a smile as co-workers congratulated her on her summary of a three-year plan for their Shared Services Center. As she followed them into the hallway, she felt numb instead of elated at the positive reaction to her hard work. Questions she had been asking herself lately came to mind again.

Where was her excitement at rising to the challenge?
Why didn't she feel that same feeling of success that she used to?

At the record-breaking age of 30, she was promoted to associate director at the Center and her paychecks came with reassuring regularity from a large American company. It was not an easy ride for her to get to the top. There were people who did not believe in her and questioned her capabilities. In the poor village she left behind, the definition of security was getting a good job in a big company. She not only succeeded in doing that, but she now had everything she dreamed of as a child, including a condo in an expensive district of Makati and a top of the line car.

This morning, she had wired her mother money to pay for a new stove and oven after the old one conked out. Elena was glad that she could afford to help above the monthly allowance she sent home to provide her mother with a comfortable life. After all, without her mother's hard work and encouragement, Elena would not have been where she was now.

Back at her desk, Elena turned on her laptop to revise the presentation. As the screen lights up, she continued to swivel on her seat. An insistent voice in her head told her to focus.

She worked 10 to 12-hour days to get this job. She was willing to do whatever it took.

But now that she had the position, along with the lifestyle she always longed for — fashionable clothes, the ability to enjoy fine dining or go for drinks with colleagues — a feeling of restlessness still overtook her at times.

Like the all-consuming poverty in her childhood that limited her in so many ways, she increasingly felt stifled by her work duties and the constant pressure to achieve. It's a new life with different surroundings and people, but one thing remained the same.

Feeling trapped and sometimes feeling lost.

The ringing phone interrupted her thoughts. John Smith, her functional manager at their U.S. headquarters wanted to touch base with her on the presentation. After Elena told him about her earlier feedback, he said he would email her a few more suggestions. He expected her to send him the final version before she left the office today since she was flying to Panama tomorrow for the conference.

"I'd like you to deliver the final presentation to our top management next week. It'll be good exposure for you. Feel up to it?" he asked.

Elena swallowed hard, picturing harsh lights, men in business suits and dozens of eyes scrutinizing the young Filipina who had somehow made it through the ranks. She knew how to play the game, she was always on top, but somehow, she didn't feel the excitement.

"I'll do my best." She respected his professionalism and hoped she wouldn't let him down. "Thanks for the opportunity. I'll see you in Panama."

After the call was over, Tina, one of her direct reports, stopped by her desk. She was in her late thirties, had two kids and was recently separated from her husband. It was no secret that she was looking to replace him. She often urged Elena to find someone, too, because, at 31, she was not getting any younger.

"Don't forget, tonight's the big night," she said with a wink. "We're meeting for dinner at the Shangri-La at nine."

"I have to stay a little longer to work on the presentation," Elena said. "But I'll be there."

Every Friday night, she and her colleagues frequented local hot spots. Going out started to become a means to de-stress and to escape the numbing series of expectations and responsibilities.

That evening, Andreas, a German investment banker friend of Tina's brother, was joining them for dinner. Tina had asked Elena multiple times to go on a double date, so at some point, she had to say yes. Tonight was the night. She had no expectations and would go with the flow.

She had met a few men, but it always ended after two or three dates. She was not in a rush but was looking forward to having a serious relationship at some point, someone she could share her success with.

She performed one final check of her presentation draft, attached it to an email, and sent it to John.

"Okay Elena time to wrap up the week and unwind a bit before your crucial presentation next week. You can do it," she said aloud.

As she shut down her laptop, she looked around the room of her office. She realized she had come a long way and she still had a long way to go.

She thought of how far she had come and how she had achieved what she always dreamed of, but she was fearful of her next move. Was she ruining her life by following expectations, conventions and going with the flow?

She arrived at Shangri-La a bit late. Elena always admired Shangri-La's beauty when she visited. It was a five-star hotel adorned by expensive chandeliers and shining marbles gracing the lobby giving a sophisticated ambiance. Six smartly dressed receptionists greeted guests for check-in and check-out. There was a bar on the left side of the lobby filled with tables and chairs. The comfortable long and short sofas on the right side of the lobby served as a waiting area for guests. The hotel offered different types of restaurants, from a buffet of different cuisines to specialized and contemporary cuisine. There was a pool bar with a matching garden situated at the right-wing of the hotel. Tonight, they had a reservation in one of the expensive restaurants serving contemporary cuisines.

Tina and three others from her team, Jennifer, Donna, and Ryan had already started drinking. A vacant seat beside

Andreas, her date for the evening, was waiting for her. She forced a smile and went straight to the vacant seat.

"Hi, I'm Elena." She extended her hand for a handshake. "Hi, I'm Andreas. Nice to finally meet you. I've heard a lot of great things about you. And by the way, you actually look different from your picture than in person."

"In what way?" Elena asked. "I think you look more dolled up in pictures than in person," Andreas said. "Either way, you look nice tonight, although you seem a bit tired."

"Yeah, I have to finish a presentation because I'm flying to Panama tomorrow for a business conference." Elena wondered what Andreas meant by pointing out that she was more dolled up in pictures than in person. Obviously, she tried to find the best angle in photos, and she wants to look good.

"Do you come here often?" Andreas said. "The ambiance is nice, but I believe the menu is overrated. Sure, this is a five-star restaurant, but I think the quality of the food is the same as regular restaurants."

"Just occasionally. I work hard so I believe I deserve a treat for myself once in a while," Elena replied.

"I noticed it's a common thing here in the Philippines to splurge in nice and fancy restaurants even if the majority of them cannot really afford the menu," Andreas expressed as he reached his almost empty cocktail drink.

"I haven't noticed that, but we do want to celebrate once in a while," Elena lied, not wanting to admit the truth to someone so arrogant.

"I've been living here in Manila for two years and noticed

that Filipinos love fancy things and have that behavior of displaying it or showing off - to be exact. Like the addiction to post everything on social media," Andreas continued.

"Is that so?" Elena was starting to get uncomfortable with the conversation.

"Yes, I think so. Like in the office, there are people buying expensive bags, shoes, and gadgets and pay it by installments. Others even save just to buy these expensive things, and I don't understand. Poor mentality and poor way of life."

Elena's phone rang. It was her mother.
"Can you excuse me a bit? I have to take this call." She stood up and answered the phone. Her mother thanked her for the stove and oven. She expressed excitement about learning how to bake with her new oven. Elena felt grateful that she could give her mother the small happiness that money can buy. Listening to her mother's voice made her feel a bit of sadness that her demanding job prevented her from being able to spend much time with her mother. Elena tried to fill in her absence with these small gifts from time to time.

She returned to her seat after her call.

"Do you normally take phone calls while talking with other people? I just find it strange," Andreas said as soon as she sat down.

"Not really, but it's my mother so I need to pick it up." Elena changed the topic. "So, tell me what made you land here in Manila?"

"I was sent here to grow the portfolio of our branch. I

didn't really want to come here because I saw on the media that Philippines is a slum. I grew up in a nice country in a sheltered family and never really experienced living in a third world country."

"So why did you accept the job if you were not interested in living in a poor area?" Elena asked.

"Well, the money is good. Save a bit then go somewhere else. It doesn't hurt," Andreas replied. Andreas searched around the restaurant with his eyes. "So, I thought this was a five-star restaurant. Why is the waiter not here yet? It has been 30 minutes since they delivered the drinks, and I am ready for my order. Is this how slow the service is here? I am not paying such high prices for this type of mediocre service, you know."

"I think the waiter will come in a minute or so," Elena replied trying to compose herself and not say anything harsh. This guy had complained as soon as she sat down beside him and never stopped. *Seriously, this is the last thing I want to hear after a tiring day. God, this is whining non-stop. If this guy does not stop complaining, I will have to leave soon. And yes, this will be the last time I will go on an arranged date. Too much effort and too time-consuming. It is making me hate my life more.*

"Elena, we are going to Euphoria after this. I will not accept no for an answer," Tina exclaimed cutting off her thoughts.

"Well, let's see how the night goes," Elena said.

"Oh, Euphoria! I heard it's overrated and overpriced. I might not join you guys," Andreas exclaimed with conviction.

Elena gave a deep sigh, relieved that this annoying guy

would not join. She wanted to escape as soon as possible. This was supposed to be her night to unwind, not to hear somebody whining. Life was testing her patience. She was silent for a moment with her brain traveling in a third dimension, asking herself so many questions.

I don't want to have all my Friday nights like this. It's so shallow and meaningless. I want a deep conversation, but it seems impossible to find somebody I can connect with, even with friends. Am I weird or am I just different? This is not the life I have envisioned myself having after all. I cannot continue like this—working, partying, and going on meaningless dates. It's the same monotonous routine. I'm starting to feel like a robot. I have achieved everything I wanted as a kid, but something does not feel right. I need to do something different, but I don't know where to start. I don't even know what it is.

"Ma'am what would you like for an appetizer?" the waiter interrupted Elena's thoughts.

"Ah, I will just have the main course. I will go for the steak, medium done. Thank you."

Thirty minutes passed by and their order arrived.

"Can you take a picture of us?" Jennifer asked the waiter. They moved to get closer to each other to fit in the lenses. Tina and Jennifer tried to find their best angle, takes after takes, reviewing the picture after every shot. Andreas gave the same cold smile for every click looking bored at what seemed to be a photoshoot rather than just a simple group photo. Elena gave a simple smile and did not bother to find the best angle. She was not in the mood for a Facebook photoshoot.

After the picture was taken, Jennifer opened her Facebook and uploaded the photo. "Did you just upload our photo?

Tag me please," Tina said.

"I just did," Jennifer responded.

"That's what I mean by Filipinos being social media addicts." Andreas insulted with a laugh.

Elena did not bother to join the conversation; she savored the dish trying to concentrate on her meal to avoid further conversation with Andreas. She had no energy to continue discussing.

Growing up, she never had the luxury to eat in nice and fancy restaurants. She was lucky enough if she could eat meat once in a while. This was one of the things she was grateful for, the ability to afford a nice meal and actually being served. Their orders arrived stunningly plated like pieces of artwork. The aroma of freshly cooked food filled the entire table. Elena's steak was stirred to perfection. The mashed potatoes looking creamy and intense, and the asparagus beautifully bathing in a beurre blanc sauce. Small edible flowers in different colors were artistically sprinkled on the plate. She sliced the beef and put it in her mouth. She closed her eyes and savored her first bite. She tasted the mashed potato and asparagus with the beurre blanc sauce, it was delicious. She proceeded to combine the three and put it in her mouth. The flavor combination burst in her mouth teasing her taste buds to go for more.

She could not imagine how she survived poverty, but now that she could afford to pay for great meals and buy the things she desired, she was grateful.

They reached Euphoria, a high-end club that charged 1000 pesos for cover. It sounded like a small amount, but this could buy a decent meal for an average family. Sometimes she felt guilty about this type of spending.

They all brought their clothes in from the parking garage and used the hotel's bathroom to change into their clubbing attire. It had been a tradition in their office to bring clubbing attire every Friday night, just as much as it had become a ritual to go clubbing and get wasted. The club was 100 square meters, with a few tables by reservation only with minimum consumption of 10,000 pesos per night. It was slick, modern, and adorned with flashy lights bright enough to light the dark place giving it a vibe. The place was full as usual, and there was a long line to get to the entrance. It took them an hour to get inside the club. Elena and her team hit the bar as soon as they entered the club.

Deep inside, she found this place pretentious and more of a status symbol rather than fun. However, she wanted to unwind tonight. She wanted to forget all those thoughts lingering in her head. She wanted to forget her upcoming business conference. She wanted to stop thinking about her responsibilities and all the expectations. She wanted to get lost in oblivion even if for just a moment.

They had shots, cocktails, and more cocktails. They shouted over the music and danced like it was the last days of their lives. For a moment, Elena achieved what she wanted to achieve for the night; to get lost in oblivion.

A thousand pistons hammered at Elena's temples when she woke up on Saturday morning. How many drinks did she consume last night? She had promised herself repeatedly that she would no longer drive while under the influence, but she had again broken her vow. Thankfully she made it home safely.

She reached for a bottle of water and went bottoms up. Over the years she learned that water was still the best natural cure for a hangover. She had to get ready for her trip, but the headache made her thinking fuzzy. She needed to pack her stuff, but she was starving, and her terrible headache was not helping her think clearly.

She ordered Chinese takeout and then sat with the delivery on her terrace. It overlooked the high-rises in metro Manilla adjacent to the slums.

The contrast was stark in the morning light; the worn-out buildings with their sagging roofs were shadowed by their tall neighbors. The cityscape seemed to represent her life, both the poverty and the relative affluence she now enjoyed. Yes, she had come a long way, but something was missing.

Suddenly she remembered that she needed to call Christina, her best friend since university days.

"Maria Elena Victoria Linares!" the other woman exclaimed when she picked up. "I can't stand the suspense. How was your date last night?"

Elena rolled her eyes. "A disaster. Andreas is the most critical man I ever met. He found fault with everything. The service was too slow, the meal too cold. I'm sure I was not up to his standards either."

"You attract what you vibrate," Christina said. "You've always been hard on yourself, wanting to be the best at whatever you do. I'm not surprised you met someone to reflect that."

"How do I change things? I always end up with the wrong guys."
Elena heard a long sigh. "You need to relax and let things happen. All you do is work."

"I'm tired of my job," Elena said. "I feel like I'm on a treadmill, putting in so many hours just to maintain my lifestyle. But what else can I do?"

Christina did not hesitate. "Find something meaningful to do."

Easy for her to say! She was married to her childhood sweetheart and had already started a family. Elena felt a stab of envy, not because her friend had an easier life, but because she was happy with the choices she made.

Not wanting the conversation to be only about her, she asked, "So what's new on your end? Anything exciting?"

Christina laughed. "Yes, if you call a leak under the bathroom sink exciting. My father's coming over this morning to fix it. It helps to have a plumber in the family."

How comforting it must be to have a father to turn to. Hers was an alcoholic who left. She never had the experience to grow up with a father. All she remembered from those early days was shouting in the house, doors slamming, and watching her mother cry.

Whenever she saw Christina with her dad, she felt a little empty inside.

How she wished she had a father growing up. How she wished she had somebody to call dad, someone who would be there to listen and help when needed. She wondered if her life would have been different if she had grown up with a father.

She glanced at the time. "I have to pack. I'm leaving this afternoon for a conference in Panama."

"When was the last time you had a holiday?" When Elena didn't answer, Christina continued, "Why don't you take a few days off afterwards? Do some sightseeing?"

"By myself?" Elena was not comfortable traveling alone. She assumed that traveling should be with someone, with people, with friends and family. Although, maybe it would be good to travel alone. She could unwind and relax without expectations from others. She thought of her many overtime hours and untaken vacation. Before she could say another word, she heard a thin wail on the phone.

"Zach just woke up, and I need to breastfeed him," Christina said. "Have a safe trip. And think about what you want."

That's the problem. Although Elena was no longer satisfied with the routine of her days or with her material possessions, she had no clue where to go from here. She felt this deep voice inside her head and deep emotion inside her heart to break free, but she didn't know what else to do outside the corporate world. She was scared to go outside her comfort zone, but at the same time, she felt that she would die of boredom on this meaningless journey if she didn't. She battled different thoughts and emotions inside her.

Her taxi arrived just after she finished preparing herself. She took her bag and luggage, look around her apartment, reached for the door and headed to the elevator. The taxi driver greeted her and immediately put her luggage in the trunk. It was a two-hour ride to the airport; the traffic was horrible. She arrived at the airport with just enough time to check-in, pass the security and board. Luckily, she had a business class ticket which allowed her to skip the long lines.

She sat on her assigned seat in the business class. She started to feel comfortable as the flight stewardess offered her a good glass of champagne.

She sighed thinking it would be a long flight, but she was satisfied with the comfort of sitting in a reclining chair with her own television screen and having meals served to her. This was better than the economy seats.

She remembered the first time she took a business class. Ignorance was written all over her face, but she tried to play it cool. She didn't know how to operate the television on her pod, but she observed how her neighbor operated the television. She was overwhelmed with the service and the VIP treatment, but she had become accustomed to it. Now it was normal for her to feel the luxury of a business class seat.

"Ah the luxury of business class," she murmured.

"I know." An old woman's voice came out of nowhere. She turned around and realized it was the old woman sitting to her left in the middle seat. She sat next to an old man who seemed to be her husband.

"Yeah, it will be a long flight, but this seat makes me relax and feel comfortable," Elena said.

"Absolutely. We are heading back home to the States, so it will be a really long flight," the old woman replied.

"Oh, you're from the States. Are you here in Philippines for holidays?" Elena asked.

"Yeah, we were here for 2 weeks. We were actually on a world tour and the Philippines was our last trip. Now we are headed back home," the husband said.

"Oh, that's nice. Where have you guys been?" Elena asked.

"We started in Latin America, then off to Europe, and here to Asia," the old woman replied.

"Yeah, we went to places we've never been. We used to travel a lot for business and vacations. Now that we just retired, we made it a point to go to places we've never been. Mostly the not so touristic places," the husband replied.

"Oh, that's really amazing. So, what kept you busy in all the years prior to retirement?" Elena asked.

"I was a psychiatrist. I specialized in women's health, treating them for psychological issues and depression," the old woman replied.

"I worked in a car manufacturing company. I was basically in charge of quality control," the old man replied.

"Oh, that's interesting. It's actually two opposite jobs that are non-related."

"Oh dear, yes but that's the beauty of it. We worked on

what we were passionate about, but at the same time, the difference in our jobs brought interesting topics for us to talk about. Although we don't normally talk about work at home," the old woman replied while sipping a glass of champagne.

"Sorry for asking a lot of questions but you got my interest. What was the love story?"

"It was the last spring break before graduation. Normally you spend spring break with friends partying, but I decided to take a vacation to San Diego to enjoy the beach and nature. One afternoon, I was at the beach reading a book when Pete asked me for sunblock. He was all red and sunburned from the scorching heat. My sunblock was on the table, so I told him to just go grab some. Then we started talking and we found out we were staying in the same hostel. I was a shy kid growing up, so I stayed in a hostel hoping to meet new friends and get over my shyness. Anyway, so that night, he invited me to dinner, and we had a great time. We realized we had so many things in common, and that we shared the same perspective about life. We parted ways after that vacation. A few years passed, and we never had a single communication. I moved to Minnesota from Boston for a job. One afternoon, I was walking, and then I bumped into Pete. We grabbed a coffee, and I realized he also moved to Minnesota for a job in the car manufacturing industry. We started to talk like it was only yesterday that we were laughing and enjoying our vacation in San Diego. The rest is history. It was destiny that brought us back together," said the old woman.

"That's really a lovely story. So, you believe in destiny?" Elena asked.

"Absolutely! There is no such thing as accident or a

coincidence, everything that happens in our lives is synchronicity. People come into our lives for a purpose and reason. I met Dorothy, my wife, for a purpose and reason. It's written in my destiny, it's destiny that made us sit in the same flight," Pete, the old man quickly answered.

"It's the same thing for me, it's my purpose to help women overcome any issues, problems, or depression they are facing. I had clients who had been battered wives for years and they stayed in that situation because of fear. I helped them understand that they have an option in life if only they are willing to open their eyes and see the bigger picture. I have clients who had been depressed because they were in series of bad relationships, and I helped them overcome their fears, transform their perspective, and help them become a better version of themselves," Dorothy replied.

"Wow!" Elena was lost for words.

"You see sometimes we are forced to stay in a situation because of fear. Fear that society will judge us, fear that our friends and families will judge us. Fear of rejection, fear of failure, and fear that we do not have any options. But what we are not aware of is that these circumstances happen because of our belief system, which is a product of what is the norm in the society or what is taught to us when we were kids. The truth is, we create our own reality. What we see in our physical world emanates from our inner world," Dorothy said.

"Absolutely! This belief system is also true for men. I can speak on that for myself working in a car industry mostly dominated by men. We work hard because we are seen as providers for our family. We are expected to feed our family, and we are seen as weak if we are at home doing the household chores instead of working and building a successful career," Pete immediately added to Dorothy's statement.

"Well, I guess this type of pressure from society exists all over the world and not just in Philippines," Elena said.

"Oh dear, absolutely! See how they expect women to be pretty, skinny and smart? See all these advertisements and how they have commercialized beauty? The advertisement world has polluted the standards of beauty by making us believe that those women in magazines, which is by far the product of air touch and superficial living, is the standard of beauty," Dorothy exclaimed.

"I agree with you. Advertisements are good, but it tampers with the basic essence of how a woman and man are projected in our society. In Philippines, if you're dark-skinned with frizzy hair and a bit chubby, you're regarded as ugly. Women are dying to have a white color. They're applying any product that would make their skin white and going to salons to get blonde, silky hair. I know it's crazy but it's the truth," Elena said. She thought about how she was once that chubby dark-skinned girl with frizzy hair, but much had changed. Thanks to the occasional glutathione injection, her dark skin had become lighter. She wore her professionally straightened hair in a bob, and her expensive clothing always looked classy and sophisticated on her fit frame.

"See, me and Dorothy share the same philosophy—to live our lives the way we want it to be. We don't listen to what people tell us to do. We taught our kids the same philosophy, and we are happy with our simple lives," Pete added.

Elena started reflecting as the conversation kept going. Maybe the couple was right, everything happens for a reason and there is no such thing as coincidence. She didn't become successful in the corporate world by a matter of coincidence or luck, she worked hard for it. And as for following society's standard, it was still a debate within her.

"Where are you going?" Pete asked, interrupting her thoughts.

"I'm going to Panama for a week for a conference," Elena replied.

"Oh, Panama! What a lovely place. A true contradiction between richness and poverty."

"It's my first time there," Elena answered.

"We went there on our world trip then headed to Cali in Colombia, then Santo Domingo in Ecuador, then Pisco in Peru. We went to non-famous and non-touristic places. We went to La Paz in Bolivia, Antofagasta in Chile, and the last was Mar Del Plata in Argentina," Pete added.

"Yes, we actually loved Mar del Plata in Argentina. It has preserved its history, but at the same time it has kept up with the modern world which makes it a unique and beautiful city. The people are so nice and sweet. There are nice restaurants along the coastline to grab a coffee, watch the sunset, and reflect. The people are welcoming to tourists and very happy to share their culture and heritage. It's a nice place to visit because it gives you a sense of history and evolution complementing each other." Dorothy's eyes were in a dreamy state as she remembered their vacation in Mar del Plata.

"It's like life, our history is our base for evolution, but it doesn't stop there," Pete added.

"We met one young couple in Mar del Plata who became our friends in our short stay. They invited us to their home twice, which is 30 minutes away from the city center. They have a small apartment, but it was so nice of them to invite us. They cooked some local Argentinian food for us. They shared their culture, their history, their family. We really had a great time sharing a meal and talking with them," Dorothy continued.

Elena tried to digest all the wisdom imparted to her in the past few hours from this wonderful couple. She told herself it was her lucky day because she met these two wonderful people who were willing to share their wisdom about life. Elena transferred their positivity towards life into her own life. She felt encouraged to follow her heart's desire and live her life. She felt a bit of relief, but at the same time, she felt that it may be too good to be true.

She started to wonder. What was her heart's desire? She had gotten lost along the way as she breathed success. She felt that she lost her identity and the connection to her own being as she enjoyed the superficial life and the momentary happiness that money brought her. She started to ponder.

"Dear, I know what you're thinking right now. Rest assured you will find your true heart's desire. You need to learn how to quiet your mind, disregard logic for a moment, follow your heart, listen to your instinct, and connect to your inner self," Dorothy said as she watched Elena pondering in silence.

"Yeah, our conversation in the last hour made me think," Elena replied. "A few months ago, I started to question whether I'm on the right track, or if I am just living somebody else's dream. And now that we are talking, these thoughts are again lingering in my head."

"It's alright. That's a good sign. Awareness is the first step and you just had it. It's not an easy process, but the journey along the way will lead you to the right path and the right direction. We will not bother you now. We have a few hours left before we land, so we will try to grab some sleep," Dorothy said.

 "Yes, I want to grab some sleep too because I know I'll need the energy," Elena replied.

"Ok, have a good rest," Pete exclaimed.

"Thank you to both of you. Thank you for sharing your story. As you said, it's destiny that made us sit next to each other on the same flight. It's probably one of those signs for me to be able to know the next step so I can find my own calling," Elena replied.

"Yes. Have a good nap, and we wish you success," Dorothy and Pete exclaimed with genuine smiles.

"Thank you. It was a great pleasure talking to both of you and I hope we can cross paths again someday," Elena replied.

"Don't mention it. It's written!" Dorothy said.

They all turned off their lights as they tried to grab a quick nap before they reached their destination.

4 LEAP OF FAITH

It was the moment of truth. It was time for Elena to deliver her presentation – the presentation she worked hard for. She stood and walked in front of the big conference room. She had done so many presentations in her life and she knew she could deliver a good presentation, but she still felt butterflies in her stomach.

The conference room was bigger than their usual conference room in Manila. The atmosphere was all business; the room was filled 60 of her colleagues from different countries all over the world, all dressed smartly. It was attended by top management all over the world. This would be a good exposure for Elena's career development. A lot of her colleagues were so envious that she got picked for the trip. Most Filipinos would love to go and visit Latin America as it's an exotic destination for them.
There was a big monitor in the front of the room with the first slide of her presentation projected. She walked slowly towards the stage, inhaling deeply. Her hands shook a bit, and she tried to give a smile as she glanced at her colleagues on the way to the stage.

She never felt nervous like this during presentations. It was probably the big conference room or the different nationalities making her uncomfortable. Maybe she was afraid to be judged, or maybe she was scared to disappoint her boss. There were so many emotions lingering deep inside her before she reached the stage, but she needed to quiet her mind of all these emotions. Today was not the day to ponder, she needed to deliver a good presentation. On the other hand, her brain was asking what was in it for her anyway. Yes, she had a high paying job, but was this something she wanted to do for the rest of her life?

"Calm down Elena, this is not the time to ponder. This is

the time to shine," she murmured to herself.

Elena reached the stage. She cleared her throat and said, "Good morning." She started her presentation a bit uneasy, but two minutes later she found the momentum and -the confidence level she always had. She was dominating the stage with her presentation and her presence.

"Thank you" it was the last slide, she just finished her presentation

The room was filled with a round of applause. Elena just finished her presentation on the three-years vision of Manila Shared Service Center. She glanced at her boss; John was all ears and smiling. Elena could feel the pride and satisfaction written in her boss' expression.

John approached her after the presentation and congratulated her on a well-done presentation.

"Elena I am so proud of you. That was a very smart, convincing and well-done presentation. Thank you for all the hard work. I know I have been so demanding lately, but I also know you deserve a bit of time off after working so hard in preparation for this event. Do not hesitate to take a few days off here in Panama. You deserve it," John said with his eyes full of pride.

"Thanks, John." Elena excused herself after the quick exchange. He was finally allowing her to take some days off. She must have really made him very proud. It was her original intention to ask him for a few days off. She already mentioned this to her boss in Manila and she got approval. She applied for two visas; Brazilian and Argentinian visa, she knew she couldn't visit these two places with a few days off but decided to get both visas

anyway. In the end, she decided to finally not take a few days off. She felt exhausted.
It would be a cool idea to take a few days off, but a few days is not enough for me to reflect. I need at least a few months for that. A few months off, in my dreams."

Elena's flight was scheduled to depart on Saturday at noon. Her average sized suitcase was all packed and ready to head back to Manila. After contemplating, she decided to go back home after the conference instead of taking a few days off as John suggested, and as she originally intended.

She arrived at the airport at 8:30 in the morning. She was a bit early and the check-in counter was still closed. She sat on the airport bench just in front of the departure screen. It was a busy Saturday morning; people from different walks of life waiting, walking, and running to catch their flights. Elena was thinking about being on a flight for nearly two days. Just the thought of it made her tired.

She looked at the departure screen and saw a flight to Buenos Aires at noon, the same time as her flight to Manila. She remembered the old couple she spoke with on the flight from Manila to Los Angeles, her connecting flight to Panama, and how they loved Mar del Plata. The name appealed to her. Mar del Plata. In English, Sea of Silver.

She remembered the old couple's story of how they met and of the young couple who invited them into their home to share their culture and food.

She thought it would be nice to learn culture and customs from other people while sharing food. She traveled a lot, but it was always either for business or holidays to touristic places. Argentinian cuisine certainly sounded nice. But well, life needed to go on. Elena stared at the departure screen.

There was something deep inside her that wanted to visit the place. She could take a few days off. Maybe she could go to Mar del Plata for a few days. But then she felt like that was something a tourist would do. She wanted to be able to explore and ponder for a bit. She wanted to stay in Mar del Plata for at least 3 months. She wanted her world to stop for a moment so she could reflect on that missing piece of life that haunted her.

The desire to go to Mar del Plata was growing deep inside, and her heart pounded. She really wanted to go to Mar del Plata, but if she did, what would she tell her boss? How would she convince her boss to give her three months' leave after delivering a superb presentation on the Manila Shared Service Center vision? Who would take on her role while she was away? What would people think of her if she just went on holiday for three months without any warning? She had a good reputation for being structured, responsible, and delivering results. Was she willing to jeopardize that image? Would she have a job to come back to if she took three months off? She could afford three months off, but it would be a lot of money to spend. What if she got fired after this and she had spent all her money on this little adventure? There were so many thoughts and emotions battling in her head and heart. Her brain rationalized that this was the craziest idea to do while her heart was telling her that taking the time off was the best decision to make.

"Follow your heart." She remembered the advice Dorothy gave while they were on the plane.

After deep contemplation, she took a deep breath, closed her eyes, and headed to the customer service counter to inquire about a plane ticket to Mar del Plata. She was directed to a Latin American airline where she could buy the ticket. She went right away, no turning back, and purchased a one-way ticket to Buenos Aires. There was no direct flight to Mar del Plata.

She searched for a Wi-Fi connection to google the best route to Mar del Plata. She was happy with how technology had evolved enough to where she could find answers to her questions immediately. A quick search revealed that Mar del Plata was four hours by bus from Buenos Aires. "I didn't realize it's that far. This is what happens with impulsive decision making, but too late for regrets. I already bought the ticket," Elena murmured.

She gave a deep sigh and began her search for a bus and a place to stay once she arrived. She opened Airbnb and found a modest apartment that she booked for three months. Her fingers were typing non-stop. She managed to arrange everything in 1 hour. She thought again about how Technology had really made things easy, possible, and accessible no matter where you are in the world. She could not imagine how this would be possible without internet. She was also happy that economy sharing had boomed in the traveling world. It made traveling a bit cheaper compared to staying in a hotel. This new concept was breaking the traditional business model, and she was thankful this had become a trend. But well, that was the least of her concerns now. She was taking an adventure and fear and excitement overwhelmed her.
She was nervous, excited, scared, and even felt a bit lost, but at the same time, she had finally found a way to escape.

"Elena, you're doing something dangerous and playing with the unknown," she said to herself. But deep inside her, there was a burning desire to take a leap of faith and just let go of all her reservations.

She was leaving behind a big responsibility and breaking the trust of all the people who respected and had high expectations of her. She needed to act professionally for the crazy decision she just took. She opened her email outlook and decided to compose two emails: one for her American boss and one for her Filipino boss. She typed out the email, explaining that since John suggested that she could take some days off and since Grace, her boss in Manila, approved her to take few days off, a request she did prior to her trip, she decided to extend her vacation. She detailed how she had worked hard in the last few years and had made great contributions to the company. She ended the email by stating that it's time for her to take all the holidays she never took, to take a break, and get some fresh ideas and new concepts and ideas to bring back to the company. She tried to convince them that this three-month sabbatical leave would bring something good for her, and hopefully, she would bring more great things to the company. "This is not very convincing, but it's worth it to try to rationalize," she said to herself.

She nominated Tina as her acting substitute while she was on holiday. She expressed her confidence that Tina would be a good fit and could carry on her duties while she was away.

She composed two more emails for her team explaining the same.

She closed her eyes after sending the last email and told herself this was it! She was up for the craziest adventure in life but no turning back. She hoped this crazy decision was all worth it and that there was a life to go back to after this.

After her flight, a four-hour bus ride, and a taxi ride, she landed in her new home for the next three months. The Airbnb host greeted her and explained to her in broken English every corner of the apartment she needed to know.

The apartment was 40 square meters with one bedroom. The living room contained a comfortable looking floral print covered sofa, a small table, and a medium-sized television. There was a small dining table with four chairs in the dining room. The kitchen was medium-sized, with a four-burner stove, an oven, a microwave, and cabinets that stored the plates, glasses, and cookware. It had a small terrace with a sea view. The shower had a bathtub perfect for a bubble bath after a long day. Overall, the apartment gave her the basics she needed for her three months stay. It was not as luxurious as her apartment, but she started to feel comfortable in her temporary home.

It was February, almost the end of summer in Argentina, and there wasn't a lot of tourists left. It was almost sunset, so she had no time to enjoy the beach. She decided to go out to find a restaurant where she could have her dinner. Tomorrow would be a new day, a day to figure out what to do.

She walked and finally found a nice restaurant just one block from her apartment. It's a typical tapas kind of restaurant in Argentina. The restaurant was almost empty with two waiters standing in front of the bar and a bartender standing behind the counter. There were eight tables with a few customers. They smiled as she entered the restaurant. She sat at a small table close to the window but far from other people. She needed her moment of silence. Two tables from her table, there was a young couple with a daughter around four-years-old. The father was feeding fries to his daughter while she obligately opened her mouth. She giggled as she enjoyed her food. The scene brought her back to her childhood memories, only this was contrary to what she grew up with. She never had that experience with her father. She could only remember her father shouting at her in his drunken state. She thought about how lucky it would be to have somebody you could call dad. She dismissed the thought and proceeded to order from the waiter.

She ordered empanadas; a savory cookie also baked in Philippines. She took a bit and closed her eyes. The empanadas were so good, but it tasted different from the ones she had in Philippines.

She ordered a steak, a must for a country like Argentina, a bit of salad, and two glasses of wine. She savored every bite of the steak. She had eaten in many fancy restaurants, but the quality of the Argentinian beef was just superb. The meat melted in her mouth and the wine complimented the taste of the beef. For the first time in her life, she ate in a way that felt like she was making a connection and relationship with the food.

She pondered over the irony of life. She had eaten in fancy restaurants to satisfy that craving for inclusion in high-end society, but the food here was so simple which made it delicious. She laughed to herself. Fancy things might not be the best sometimes, and this simple meal was one of the best she had so far.

After a fulfilling meal, exhaustion finally set in. She decided to end the day early. She headed back to her new apartment, cleared her head, and went to sleep.

5 MEETING THE GURU

Elena woke up in an unfamiliar environment. After a few minutes, she realized she was in Mar Del Plata, Argentina.

"Oh God Elena, what have you done?" she asked herself. An inner voice answered her. "It's the best decision you've made in life so far. You're smart and you can figure it out."

She got up and walked out on her terrace overlooking the beach. She inhaled the morning breeze and told herself, yes, this was the best decision she had ever made. She closed her eyes and enjoyed the cool breeze, the sunshine kissing her cheeks, and the waves sounding like music to her ears.

Alright Elena, what's next? You need to do a program. This is a soul-searching holiday and not just a lazy holiday. She went back inside and headed towards the kitchen and prepared coffee with a simple breakfast. It was a good idea that she did her grocery shopping yesterday.

She couldn't explain it, but she felt calm and relaxed. She took a quick shower then put her bikini underneath her shorts and tank top. Gladly, she brought the bikini she bought last summer which she never wore. She prepared her bag for the beach. She never had that confidence level to wear a bikini, but right now she didn't care. She wasn't in Philippines where people have negative things to say whenever you're wearing a bikini. It was freedom for her.

She swam like a kid, enjoyed the waves, sunbathed a bit, then headed to a small restaurant to get a drink. She felt thirsty.

She felt relaxed swimming and enjoying the beautiful sunny day. The cool breeze touched her face as she walked along the shoreline. The sun gave a tingling burn to her skin. The draft from the ocean which seemed infinite filled her lungs. She looked around and enjoyed the sights. The few people enjoying the waves. The bars and cafés lined up close to the shoreline now almost empty as the summer was almost over. The tall buildings on the other side of the city showing evidence of progress, the cars passing by on the street. The city and beach vibe gave her energy and hope that everything would be okay.

She continued to walk and finally decided to enter a small café which was almost empty. She was in the mood for a smoothie. She ordered at the bar then decided to have a seat on the terrace. On her way to the table, she noticed an old man sitting comfortably outside.

The old man was in his late sixties, dressed in summer shorts and a white short-sleeved polo. He was sitting comfortably while reading his book. On his table was an empty cup of espresso. The man seemed oblivious to his environment while he savored the pages of his book. The wrinkles adorning his face showed a sign of wisdom and knowledge. A sense of peace and happiness vibrated from his aura.

He was reading a book entitled *The Prophet* by Kahlil Gibran. She raised her eyebrows in interest. Unconsciously, she started reading the synopsis on the back cover of the book. She hadn't even noticed that she was standing in front of the old guy. The old man noticed her staring and put his book down. He smiled at her and said, "Hola."

"Hola. Buenas dias," she said in her broken Spanish. She was embarrassed to realize that she was standing in front of the old man staring and reading his book cover.

"Buenas dias, senorita. Como estas?"

"Muy bien. Sorry, that's the extent of my Spanish," Elena replied.

"You're from Philippines?" the old man asked.

"Yes, how did you know?"

"I used to travel a lot and I've been to Philippines, so I am familiar with the facial features. You also use a lot of Spanish words in the Philippines, being a Spanish colony for more than 300 years. I have to say you adopted a lot of Spanish culture," the old man replied.

"Yes, I guess so. I feel that we have lost the true Filipino culture, and it became a mixture of Spanish and American. But now it's leaning towards American."

"I am aware of that."

"You seem to know a lot of things".

"I am an old man, my beautiful senorita. Aging has taught me wisdom and traveling has opened my eyes to the world."

Elena couldn't believe it. This was her second time meeting a person full of wisdom. First, the encounter with the couple on the plane and their philosophical conversation which triggered her to take a bold step, and now this old man telling her interesting things.

With a bit of hesitation, Elena continued, "I would really love to talk with you more. Would you mind if I sit with you?"

"Be my guest, my beautiful senorita. I can see the excitement in your eyes but beneath lies fear and anxiety. There is something bothering you inside. I have a feeling that your reality is not the same as your expectations."

"Are you a psychic or a fortune-teller?"

"I told you, aging has taught me wisdom and traveling opened my eyes to understand the unknown."

"I was in Panama last week for a business trip. Instead of taking my return flight, I took a flight to Buenos Aires then took the bus here."

The old man clapped. She didn't understand why. Before she could even open her mouth to ask, the old man spoke.

"Congratulations on your first attempt to get out of your comfort zone. Society, including your family and close friends, would tell you that you're crazy and stupid. Why would you embrace such stupid decisions? But honestly, that's a brave act. By default, we start learning once we get out of our comfort zone. How long do you intend to stay here?"

"I don't know, probably three months."

"What do you intend to do in those three months?"

"Enjoy life and find myself. If lucky, find out my purpose in life."

"That sounds serious. Does that include finding love?" The old man gave a teasing smile.

"How do you know I'm single? I can probably include that, but that seems mission impossible. I'm only here for three months. I know I will leave after that."

"Well dear senorita, if you had somebody in life, you wouldn't have taken this trip to Mar del Plata alone. And who knows, you may belong here," the old man replied. "Spot on!" Elena laughed. "I would love to, but I don't think I should force it, right?" Elena gave a wry smile.

"Of course! I don't mind helping you in this journey if you want. I can be your coach, mentor, whatever you want to call it," the old man replied.

Elena contemplated a bit. She just met this old guy a few minutes ago and now he was offering to be her mentor. How could she trust a stranger in a foreign place? On the other hand, her heart was telling her to trust and let go. Everything happens for a reason.

"Please. I feel that you have so much wisdom to bestow upon me," Elena said.

"It would be a pleasure for me to help a lost soul find its purpose. Every day at noon, we will meet in this café and have our daily session. I would teach you what I learned in life."

"What do I need to pay in return?" Elena asked with a bit of hesitation. This old man was giving her terms and they had just met. Trust and let go echoed in her brain.

"Nothing. The payment is for you to learn and become enlightened."

"Okay. So, where do we start? Are you going to give an assignment? Do I need to learn to meditate? Do I start writing in a journal? Do I need to practice yoga? Do I need to answer some psychological questions?" Elena asked.

"Hold on. First lesson, learn the art of patience. Mastery takes time. You don't develop a skill overnight. That's the problem with your generation right now, everything is by click and you forgot how to do things the traditional way. Change is good but don't forget tradition." The old man smiled.

"You need to buy a journal today. Tonight, write all the things you hate, things you worry about, things that's bothering you, and any other things that make you uncomfortable. Once you're done, start writing the things that you like, things that make you smile, things that make you happy."

"Okay and then?" Elena paused.

"I just told you, learn the art of patience. I will tell you what we will do tomorrow. Finish your first assignment tonight, and tomorrow you will find out."

"Salute!" The old guy raised his empty cup of coffee for cheer with Elena.

"I have to go now. I promised my son I would join him for a late lunch today. I will see you tomorrow," the old man said.

"I am Santiago, by the way. And you are?"

"My name is Elena."

"Okay Elena, I have to go. I will meet you tomorrow. Don't stress too much. You should do your assignment with fun and love," Santiago said with a smile.

"I will." Elena gave a smile.

She started to think that this was too much of a coincidence, but then immediately realized there was no such thing as coincidence. She felt that the universe was conspiring to put the right people in her life. The couple she met on the plane were so nice and full of wisdom and now she just met an old man also full of wisdom. She smiled thinking of the great adventure ahead. She finished her smoothie and headed to the city center to buy a journal.

She saw a small shop which looked like a bookstore. She was greeted by the cashier who seemed to be the owner. The shop was small, but it had everything from books, to notebooks, to paper. It was 4 o'clock in the afternoon by then, and the shop was empty except for a tall, lean guy. The guy looked at her as she entered the shop and gave her a simple smile. Her heart pounded. The guy was absolutely gorgeous. She smiled in return. The guy walked towards the cashier carrying a journal, paid, and left.

She scanned the shop looking for a journal. She saw the same journal that the guy bought. She reached for the same one and paid the cashier for it. She left the shop feeling happy and full of energy. She was in the mood to cook, so she walked towards a supermarket. She wasn't a really good cook, but there was always time to learn. She did her groceries and headed home.

She prepared a simple meal that would serve as a very late lunch and early dinner. She reminded herself that she needed to eat properly and on time beginning tomorrow.

She opened the journal and reached for her pen. She started her list of things she didn't like, highlighting the title. She consumed three pages just writing her dislikes. She started on the next page and titled the list "things I like" then highlighted it. She started writing but paused after writing six things she liked. She realized how fast she could write the things she disliked, and how much effort it took to write the things she liked. She continued with a few pauses in between and consumed one page for the things she liked. She couldn't believe that she had more dislikes than likes. She closed her eyes and sighed, telling herself that this was probably the reason why she was unhappy.

"Don't worry Elena, after this entire adventure, you will learn how to appreciate more things, even just the simple things," she told herself.

She switched on the television and decided to watch before she went to bed.
Aside from the fact that all the channels were in Spanish, she couldn't concentrate on the television. Her brain started to travel again. She was happy with her decision to take three months' sabbatical leave, but she asked herself if she would be happy to go back to that same life. The clear answer in her head was NO. She thought about what she would do when she went back, she needed a high paying job to maintain her lifestyle. She had gotten used to this lifestyle, but she didn't want to be the same corporate slave.

She started asking herself what her passion was. Maybe she could start from there. She couldn't remember any passion. All she did was work hard and deliver results. She grabbed a pen and paper and started thinking of possible ideas of what she could do when she went back home. Thirty minutes had passed, and the paper was still empty. She surrendered at the thought. Maybe she could try some other time.

"Elena, don't be too hard on yourself. Ideas will come, let

go and trust." She put down the pen and decided to go to bed. Tomorrow would be a new day, an interesting start to a new life.

She woke up at around seven in the morning feeling refreshed and full of energy. She got up and prepared herself a coffee then changed her clothes for a quick jog along the beach.
She jogged five kilometers in 45 minutes along the shoreline. She came back to eat breakfast, took a shower, and put her swimming attire on. She swam at the beach before noon, dried off, then headed to the café to meet Santiago for her first lesson. Somehow, she found a rhythm in this adventure.

Santiago was sitting at the same table. He smiled at her as she walked towards him.

"Hola, my beautiful senorita. Como estas?" Santiago greeted her.
'Muy bien. Buenas dias." She smiled and reached toward Santiago to give him a beso, an Argentinian custom she had adopted.

They ordered coffee as soon as the waiter arrived.

"So how was your first assignment? It shouldn't have been that hard, right?" Santiago asked.
"It took me only ten minutes to finish the list of dislikes and I wrote three full pages. It took me time to finish the list of likes and I wrote only one page."
"What did you learn from that exercise?" Santiago asked.
"That I actually live in a world I don't like, and that I complain more than I appreciate."

Santiago clapped. "Well done. You understood the learning exercise. So, tell me, what was on the top of your list of dislikes?" Santiago asked.

"First: I hate how I am conforming to society. I hate that my family and friends have everything to say for every decision I make. Second: I really don't like my work. I thought it's what I really wanted, but when I was writing the things I hate, I just started writing about my job".

"Hold on, so you don't want to be a conformist," Santiago interrupted.

"As much as possible, yes," Elena replied.
"And what was the third in your list?" Santiago continued.

"I hate being single. I fear that I will end up as a spinster, but I don't want to marry a guy just for the sake of marrying. I want to marry my one true love," Elena explained.

"You want to live your life with freedom. The first thing you need to learn is to do whatever makes you happy. Easier said than done, but it's liberating. Listen to that inner voice inside you and follow your heart. Your heart will know the right answer, just try to listen. It doesn't matter if you don't conform to the norm or standards, remember you're different and you're special by your own definition. Don't let other people dictate your happiness. You take charge of your own happiness," Santiago explained.

"Wow, that's profound but you're right. I know these things from the bottom of my heart, but I just ignore it. I was eaten by the entire system and I forgot to live in my own system," Elena responded.

"Second, why would you stick to a job you don't really like?" Santiago asked.

"It gives me a sense of security," Elena replied.

"If you're working there just for the prestige and the money, forget about it. Search within you what you love to do, what you're passionate about, what you feel is your purpose. Do it and cultivate it. The money will come afterwards if you like what you're doing. Having a big house, nice cars, having a lavish lifestyle is all superficial".

"It's not like that Santiago, but well, I will let you continue." Elena protested.

"You don't need all those material things to be happy. Why do you need a big house if you're alone? What purpose would it serve? Why would you have an expensive car if having a simple one is enough to reach your destination? It's good to experience great things in life but it doesn't necessarily have to be extravagant". Santiago continued.

"I understand," Elena inserted.

"You can have a good meal in a simple restaurant and still feel full and satisfied. And you don't have to take a photo of the food and post it on your Facebook, like all the people in your generation are doing. That is not the purpose of eating in a restaurant."

Elena just laughed at Santiago's last sentence. "You're right, in this digital age, we forgot to appreciate simple pleasures because we are busy taking photos to show off on social media." The truth of Santiago's words felt like a slap to her face.

"Third: Being alone should be seen as a blessing and not as a curse. In order to find the right person, you should first be the better version of you. Once you start appreciating yourself and learning to love yourself, the universe will flow and will give you exactly what you are looking for," Santiago explained.

"Hmm, that sounds so spiritual. Does it require some kind of meditation?" Elena exclaimed unconvinced. "I am not so sure it just happens like that. I have been on several dates, but it's all shallow and meaningless conversation. I always end up dating the wrong men."

"I knew you would react exactly like that." Santiago smiled and shook his head. "But hey, you cannot have somebody perfect if you don't feel that you are perfect inside out. You cannot find somebody with great character and personality if you don't have the right character yourself. Trust that there is a reason you long for one true love".

"Is that so? I don't feel like that. I haven't found that one true love you're talking about," Elena interrupted.

"That desire is implanted in you because you have one true love out there. It will be given to us by the divine source once we are ready to accept it. Rushing into relationships not meant for us will only leave a stain on our heart to a point where we forget ourselves. Why would you go into a relationship where you don't feel right? Because you feel the pressure or fear? Whichever it is, it would not lead you to happiness. It would only lead to misery. Learn how to cultivate yourself and trust that your one true love will come. Remember the art of patience."

"Wow, I got off track there." Elena gave a dry laugh. "You sounded like a real guru saying deep things that are a bit hard for me to absorb. But I trust you, and I trust that we met for a reason."

"I think you understood what I meant. Your brain is just in denial. So, what are the other things you learned from this exercise?" Santiago asked.

"That I should start listening to my heart, follow it, and trust the timing of the universe," Elena replied.

Santiago clapped. Instead of agreeing, he would clap when he found that his point was taken.

"So, any other things? I will not ask what you like because I am sure it's the opposite of everything you have written in your three pages of dislikes," Santiago said.

Elena laughed. "Santiago, you're such a mind reader. Ok, I learned that most of the things I focused on in my life are superficial and material things. I forgot to cultivate my soul."

Santiago again clapped. "Well done, kiddo. Let's pay for the coffee. I will treat you to a good lunch in a nice restaurant, but I will have to leave you after lunch as I have personal commitments. Try to visit Mar del Plata Cathedral afterwards. I know Philippines is a Catholic country, a legacy from the Spaniards. I don't know if you're religious or not. I myself do not believe in religion, but the cathedral is a nice place to visit. The atmosphere and the artwork give a certain level of calmness."

"What commitments?" Elena asked.
"Soon you will find out. For now, just focus on our lessons," Santiago replied.
"So, what is my next lesson tomorrow?" Elena asked.

"I want you to write an appreciation journal. Write anything you appreciate. Start learning how to empty your mind and listen to the beat of your heart. While trying to clear your mind and trying to listen to your heartbeat, observe your emotions and the changes in your body,"

Santiago said.

"Ok." It was the only word Elena could utter at the moment. They just had a deep conversation, and she just had so many realizations. She felt good about this first step to enlightenment.

They paid for their coffee and started to walk. They were going to a small restaurant for a good Argentinian traditional meal. Elena was excited to try the local dishes.

They went to a small restaurant. The waiters greeted Santiago; he was well known in the restaurant. Santiago and an old man who looked like the owner gave a traditional beso.

"Ah amigo, la mesa para dos persona con esta bella dama," Santiago said in Spanish.

"Si claro, con mucho gusto," the old man replied.
Dos filetes con chimichurri con patatas fritas, mediano y."
Santiago looked at Elena, "How do you want your steak cooked?"

"Um, medium done?" Elena replied. She was expecting it traditional and fancy, but Santiago ordered a steak. She told herself to calm down and learn to appreciate.

"Bueno, mediano hecho para la bella dama," Santiago told the owner.
"Bueno, con mucho gusto." The old man replied with a smile.
Santiago looked at her. "You don't mind if I order for you, right?"

"No, not at all. I trust your judgement," Elena replied with a smile. She wanted to browse the menu, but for now, she would go with the flow.

After 15 minutes, empanadas were served. Elena was delighted to see empanadas. The one she had when she just arrived at Mar del Plata was so delicious. Empanadas were one of her favorites growing up. Another 15 minutes later after they finished their empanadas, two plates of steak and fries with a green sauce were served.

Santiago explained that the sauce was called chimichurri, a typical Argentinian sauce made of finely chopped parsley, oregano, onion, garlic, chili pepper flakes, olive oil and a touch of acid, like lemon or vinegar. At first, she thought it was just a typical steak but when she took a bite of the beef with the sauce, it was an incredible combination of flavors. She had never tried meat this tender and good, not even in the most expensive restaurants in Makati, and the sauce was just superb.

They finished lunch. Elena was thankful for this simple but delicious meal.

"I will leave you now, enjoy your walk and visit to the Mar del Plata Cathedral. Going to the church does not necessarily reaffirm your faith, but it gives a certain sense of calmness. Tell me about it tomorrow, and don't forget to finish your assignment."

"Claro!" Elena laughingly replied.

"You are a fast learner, mi bella dama. Enjoy your day! Chao." Santiago left after paying the bill.

Elena started to walk outside the restaurant to find directions to the Cathedral. It was almost 4 o'clock in the afternoon when she finally reached the Cathedral. She entered and was welcomed by pure beauty. The cathedral was built in Neogothic style with a beautiful carved wood altar, a magnificent inlaid wood floor, dramatic stain glass windows, and beautiful lighting, highlighting the beauty in every angle.

The place was not crowded. There were a few people inside, mostly tourists. She walked towards the holy water and did a sign of the cross. As she walked towards the holy water, she bumped into somebody.

"Sorry," Elena said immediately.
"It's okay," a deep voice replied.

She looked up to check who she accidentally bumped into and realized it was the same guy she saw in the shop yesterday. What a coincidence. Before she could even say a word, the guy left and kept walking.

Damn, Elena. Where did your tongue go? She told herself immediately that this was not the time to flirt. Besides, she was inside the church. This was the time to see, enjoy the view, and most importantly pray and re-affirm her faith. She had come to reflect and appreciate this historical cathedral.

She sat, closed her eyes and started to pray. She sat still after her prayer and reflecting on how her life journey was and reflecting on how her life journey would be after this adventure. She left after an hour and headed towards the beach for a walk and to watch the sunset.

As soon as she reached her apartment, she headed to the shower and changed into comfortable clothes. She grabbed her journal and started to write the things she appreciated. She couldn't believe the sudden shift. Yesterday, it was difficult for her to write things she liked and now it only took 10 minutes to write four pages. She smiled and closed her journal. She sat in a meditative position and started to meditate. It was hard for her to concentrate. The image of the guy she bumped into in the shop and Mar del Plata Cathedral kept on popping up in her head. When she couldn't concentrate after a few tries, she decided to stop.

"Okay Elena, try again tomorrow. Now time for bed," she told herself.

7 THE ENCOUNTER

She woke up and started her usual routine. Started with a coffee and a jog, changed into her swimming attire, then headed to the beach. She went for a quick swim, laid down on her beach towel, and bathed under the sun. At noon, she went to that small café to meet Santiago.

"Buenos dias, mi bella dama." Santiago welcomed her with a smile and a standard beso.

"Buenas dias, mi maestro," Elena replied.

"So, how was your trip yesterday?" Santiago asked, and before Elena could order anything, two cups of coffee came out: one expresso for Santiago and one café con leche for her.

"It was amazing. The cathedral was a pure work of art with delicate details into perfection," she answered.

"Well that's the purpose of going there, appreciating delicate details put into perfection. It's like life, the simple things we do serve as a delicate detail of our entire being," Santiago replied.

"Indeed. I was so happy. I sat there and started to learn again how to pray. I sat still and reflected on my life," Elena replied.

"That's very nice to hear. And how well did you do with your assignment?" Santiago asked.

"It was surprising that I was able to write the things I appreciate so much faster than yesterday," Elena replied.

"What did you realize?" Santiago asked

"I realized that as soon as I started to let go of my inhibitions and just embraced my present moment, I was able to appreciate even the smallest things in life," Elena explained.

Santiago clapped as usual, and Elena smiled. "You're a fast learner, what can I say?"

"Oh, thank you. I did not intend to learn fast, but everything that you're saying is just flowing into my system automatically," Elena replied.

"Good. That only means you are in the right time to embrace change and go beyond your comfort zone to seek your true purpose and happiness," Santiago explained.

"You think so?" Elena asked.

"It's not what I or you think, it's what you're experiencing right now. Try to be aware of the paradigm shift happening in your life as you go on with this adventure. You will start to embrace uncertainty. You will start feeling okay outside your comfort zone, and you will start losing your fear for the unknown."

"Okay. As I said, I trust your judgement," Elena replied.

"Tell me, what are the top things you highly appreciate?" Santiago said.

"First, I was thankful to have finally found the guts to do something bold and unconventional. This trip is a big risk for my career. I don't even know if I have a career to go back to, but I don't have any worries at all. Ironically, I feel a sense of peace and relief," Elena answered.

"That is a good realization, and I'm happy you took the leap and came to Mar del Plata instead of going back to the Philippines." Santiago laughed.

"Yeah, I know, I am crazy but it's worth it." Elena laughed as well.

"My second would be, I am very thankful I met the American couple on the plane who gave me some sort of enlightenment which pushed me to book a flight coming here. And—"

"The most important part. I am so thankful that I met a master. I met you. You have such a pearl of profound wisdom about life, and I look forward to meeting you every day."

"I should probably start charging professional fees at some point," Santiago teased.

"What? I thought this was a free service."

"I am kidding, mi bella dama. I am more than grateful meeting you here. It is of my utmost desire to share my wisdom and inspire people."

"Would you tell me something about your life and how you became so profound like this?" Elena asked.

"I will someday, but not this time. Remember the art of patience," Santiago replied with a smile.

"Ah! You're killing me, Santiago." Elena laughed. "Anyway, so the other thing in my appreciation list, was receiving a gift of intelligence and being able to capitalize on it to get out of poverty and enjoy the momentary happiness that material things could offer in life.

"That sounds so materialistic to me," Santiago interrupted.

"I know it sounds materialistic but growing up in the slums with little and working at a young age to help my mother get through our daily lives was tough. I use the gift of intelligence I received from God to advance in life. I achieved a lot at a young age. I am proud of what I've done but will be prouder if I find my true purpose and live with it."

Santiago clapped as usual. "You are a strong woman Elena. I admire your determination."

"Thank you, Santiago. The irony of it, I'm going into this same circle of struggle, the only difference is finding more meaning in life rather than achieving success," Elena replied.

"I remember meeting you two days ago with all that confusion and worry written in your face. Now I feel like I am talking to a different person," Santiago exclaimed.

"I am thankful to meet you. We just started with my lesson, but I feel like I have already learned a lot. To think about it, all you asked me to do is to reflect on my life," Elena replied.

"But that's the entire lesson. I will not teach you what you should do, but I will teach you how to listen to your heart so you will learn how to trust and follow what it says. Trust me, whatever unanswered questions we have, just silence the mind and start listening to your heart and soon you will know the answer. Our heart is the door to our inner soul," he explained

"Wow, you're really deep. Thank you for all the

philosophical explanations. I am starting to exercise that silencing the mind and listening to my heart in my daily life."

"Good. In due time, you will master it and won't even need me. You will just remember me as a good old friend who taught you how to trust yourself and the universe," Santiago replied.

"I really hope I reach that stage," Elena replied.

"Without a doubt! I will not be able to meet you tomorrow as I have a personal commitment, but I would suggest you go to Torre Tanque tomorrow," Santiago continued.

"Another personal commitment. You're mysterious sometimes," Elena teased Santiago.

"It's also good to keep some privacy in my life". Santiago smiled. "For our next meeting, write in your journal about the person you want to become after your little adventure here in Mar del Plata,"

"I am really sad that I won't see you tomorrow, but it's okay as long as I will see you the next day. Have fun with whatever personal commitments you have for tomorrow," Elena replied.

"Thank you. Enjoy Torre de Tanque and tell me about it when we meet," Santiago replied. He asked for the bill as they finished their coffee. Elena tried to reach for the bill when the waiter came out.

"Santiago please, just let me pay this time. It has been such a pleasure to spend coffee time with you."

"Thank you," he replied with a smile.

She went through her normal routine the next day and walked all the way to Torre de Tanque. It was a public water tank situated on the corner of Falucho and Mendoza, at the highest point of the Loma de Stella Maris. It was 88 meters high and the top could be accessed by elevator or climbing the 194 steps.

Elena already walked a lot during the day, so she decided to take the elevator. When she reached the view deck, she was in awe of the breathtaking view. It gave a whole view of the entire Mar del Plata. Elena slowly walked to the edge of the view deck, closed her eyes, and inhaled the breeze. She was so happy. She was on top of the world.

"Magnificent, isn't it? It gives a view of the entire city, fresh breeze from the sea, and a taste of Mar del Plata's character," Elena opened her eyes and was surprised to see the same stranger she met at the shop and the cathedral.

"Yes, I feel like I am on top of the earth. It's lovely up here," Elena quickly replied.

"I cannot explain these random meetings with you. Are you also visiting the town?" Elena added.

"No, I live here in Mar del Plata. I try to go for a walk and to visit nice places in the afternoon when I can."

"Okay. I am here for a short holiday and I'm trying to visit nice places. I met this old man, very nice and full of wisdom, a few days ago in a small café. He suggested that I visit this place."

"The locals here in Mar del Plata are really nice, polite, and welcoming. There are a lot of nice places to see. I try to visit places as much as I can to appreciate my own village," the guy replied.

"Enjoy your stay. I have to go now," the guy added.

Elena was left standing still trying to catch her breath. What a series of coincidences, in fact too many coincidences. She heard the voice of the old couple she met on the plane. "There is no such thing as coincidence, everything is synchronized."

She reminded herself to stay grounded and to not get too excited. She looked around on top of the Tower, the view was superb. There was no question why this place was called Mar del Plata "Sea of Silver." The sea was glowing like silver in its own right.

Santiago was waving and smiling as she walked towards him.

"Buenas dias, mi bella dama," he greeted as she approached the table. They had their typical beso and sat down.

"What a beautiful day. I am happy to see you," Elena mentioned.

"I am happy to see you too. How was your trip to Torre de Tanque yesterday?"

"It was amazing, and the view is superb. Thank you for your advice to visit the place."

"My pleasure! Tell me, did you finish your assignment?" Santiago asked.

"Absolutely," Elena replied.

"Tell me, what is the type of person you want to become after this little adventure of yours?"

"I want to be true to myself and to listen to my heart. I realized all through my life I was living with other people's expectations. I was listening to the noise of the world so much that I forgot to listen to the silence in my heart. I want to love myself and accept all my imperfections and insecurities.

"I see you as a confident woman, but I can sense some insecurity," Santiago interrupted.

"When I was young, I was called ugly because of my dark

skin, I used to hate my hair because it's not like the hair of those celebrities in telenovelas or that of my classmates," Elena continued.

"You haven't answered my question, mi bella dama. Have you accepted your imperfections?" Santiago insisted.

"Yes, I no longer feel the need to lighten my skin, I no longer feel the need to straighten my hair, I no longer feel the pressure to be skinny. These are not imperfections; these features are what make me unique. I am unique and I should accept that." Elena answered Santiago.

Santiago again clapping. "Continue, I am listening."

"I felt rejected and was drowning in depression because I didn't have anybody in my life right now, a situation I didn't even recognize.

"Interesting. I cannot imagine you depressed, probably confused?" Santiago stared into Elena's eyes. "Go, on"

"I realized that happiness comes from within and not from having somebody. I want to start living a healthy lifestyle. The crazy partying, I used to do in Manila will just be history now. I want to live a simple life and give up the materialistic mentality that I embraced as I changed my status in life. I want to find my inner sense and purpose. I want to become a better person every day." Elena stated in a calm and convincing way.

"It's a good realization and it's a good thing to live with who you are instead of living what people tell you to do," Santiago replied.

"When I was young, I fell in love with a beautiful and great woman. My parents did not like her, and I became rebellious. Then my actions started chaos within our home and within myself. I loved my parents, but I also loved the girl. I left Mar del Plata and went traveling in the mountains. I did some sort of meditation. I came back as a new person and I spoke to my parents. I explained to them that I loved the girl and I loved them too. They would have to trust my judgement and respect my decision. I explained to them that marrying this girl didn't mean I didn't respect them. It was a matter of following my heart. My parents gave me their blessings and I married her. We have a son we love dearly."

"Wow, that's a beautiful story. Where is your wife now?" she asked.

"She joined the creator two years ago, but I don't blame God. I was happy to have her in this lifetime, and I know at some point we will be reunited again. Some things happen for a reason, and I suppose my purpose in life is not yet complete. So here I am, talking to a young lady and sharing the lessons I learned in life." Santiago smiled.

Elena laughed at Santiago's last sentence.

"In addition, I am here for my son. He is not in a good emotional state right now. His mother died 2 years ago, and his fiancée left him 6 months ago."

"Why did she leave him?" Elena asked.

"She had a big dream and would like to pursue a career in a big city. My son wanted to stay here in Mar del Plata and cultivate his restaurant and handle the family business. They tried to make their relationship work with her in New York and him here in Mar del Plata. Neither of them wanted to compromise and move, so in the end, it did not work out," he explained.

"Oh, that's sad. The irony of life. Here I am wanting to leave a big career in a big city and trade it for a simple life, and others want the opposite." Elena smiled.

"That's the reason most of us are not happy. We fail to appreciate the simple good things we have in our lives and we always want more."

"True. I started to appreciate my life. I realized I served as an inspiration to the young generation in our village to strive harder to reach success. I realized that I also served as an inspiration to my team and my colleagues in believing that nothing is impossible. I realized that I gave strength to my mother who gave me enormous support".

"Do you think you will still serve as an inspiration after your little adventure?" Santiago challenged Elena.

"I have no idea," Elena replied.
"Do you miss the luxury?" Santiago never stopped challenging Elena.

"I realized that the material things I possessed in Manila should not be a product of materialism but a consequence of my hard work. I realized I should not be defined by labels of clothing that I wear but rather appreciate it to complement the character I became. No matter what I wear or possess, I should not let it define my life. These are pure consequences for the hard work I put into my life. The most important thing is to cultivate my soul and character because that is what defines me," Elena added.

"Bravo! In due time, I know you will become the greatest version of you without a doubt. And who knows, you could also become a guru to somebody else," Santiago added.

"Hahaha. That would be in a million years, but really, thank you."

"Bueno, my sincerest apologies if I cannot meet you tomorrow, but try to visit Torre del Monje."

For your next assignment, try to visualize your ideal life after this adventure. Tell me how you envision your new life. For now, I have to go. See you on the next day." Santiago stood and left.

9 ANOTHER ENCOUNTER

Elena arrived in Torre del Monje around 1 o'clock in the afternoon after getting lost and taking the wrong bus. She did a bit of research the night before about Torre del Monje. She learned that Torre del Monje actually means Tower of Monks in English and is one of the icons in Mar del Plata. It was built with medieval influences from a rock formation from Punta Piedras in 1904. It was formerly known as Torre Pueyrredón and was earlier called the Belvedere.

She learned that at the beginning of the 20th century, the town of Mar del Plata was defined as the favorite destination of the upper class of Buenos Aires, who built their luxury villas there to spend summer vacations in. One of the holidaymakers who belonged to the bourgeoisie was Ernesto Tornquist, an entrepreneur, and rancher, who devoted himself to numerous public works in Mar del Plata. He beautified the city and chose to establish his summer home in this place.

He endowed the place with a building that transmitted charm and intrigue to visitors and decided to finance the construction of a lookout. To give the building more mystery, he commissioned an architect to use a medieval style, recalling the old European fortresses or castles. Now this place is a famous tourist destination in Mar del Plata. It has a café-restaurant on top of the tower overlooking the entire city.

She looked around and was happy to see a small medieval type village. She felt like she had traveled to the 18th century. She closed her eyes and inhaled the breeze coming from the seaside. She walked around the shoreline for a few minutes until she noticed a familiar figure. It was the guy she kept on bumping into in tourist places she visited for the last few days. The guy smiled; he was probably thinking the same thing as Elena– coincidences.

"Well, I guess we will keep on bumping into each other every day," the guy said.

"I guess so too. Call it a coincidence. My mentor, the old man whose teaching me about life suggested that I visit this place today, and so I did," Elena replied.

"Good fortune that he suggested this place to you. By the way, I am Javier." The guy extended his hand for a handshake.
"Elena." She shook his hand.

"Since we keep bumping into each other in the last few days, would you mind if I invite you for a late lunch in the café-restaurant on top of the tower?" Javier asked.

"That's a good idea. I am starving. I took the wrong bus and it took me ages to reach here." Elena gave a simple smile trying to control her pounding heart from this excitement. She couldn't believe this gorgeous guy was asking her to join him for lunch. She kept herself grounded and told herself this was just a modest Argentinian way of hospitality.

They walked together to the elevator that led to the restaurant on top of the tower. Javier asked for a table on the terrace. They sat down, and she felt a bit uneasy. Javier was too gorgeous with his bright hazelnut eyes gleaming in the sunshine, his curly disheveled hair adding to his masculinity, and his three-day-old whiskers adding a sense of character.

"Tell me, how did you end up here in Mar del Plata?" Javier asked.

"It's a long story," Elena replied.

"Well, we have a lunch to share and I am all ears. Why don't you start from the beginning?"

Before Elena could reply, the waiter came with the menus. Elena immediately opened it to find an escape instead of telling her story to this gorgeous stranger. As she scanned the menu, she had a hard time concentrating on what to order. Her excitement and pounding heart had quelled her hunger.

"Do you need help to decide?" Javier asked with a smile.

"I am undecided. What would you recommend?"

"I suggest you try locro, it's the Argentinian national dish traditionally served during the celebration of the Argentinian May Revolution. It is a stew made of cord, beef, chorizo, and vegetables," Javier suggested.

"Ok. I would love to try a traditional Argentinian dish," Elena replied.

"Should we start with your story while waiting for the waiter to come back and take our orders? You said it's a long story so we should get started," Javier insisted with a smile.

Elena's heart pounded every time Javier smiled. She couldn't believe she was in front of this gorgeous man who looked like the main character in the telenovelas she used to watch as a kid. She was not convinced that this type of gorgeous man would be interested in her. It was too good to be true. She stopped herself from thinking and overanalyzing.

Ah, the problem with women, we overanalyze simple situations, she thought.

"I am waiting for your interesting story." Javier again smiled.

"Okay. I am not sure if my life is interesting. Anyway, I was born and raised by a single mother in a small village in the north of Philippines. My drunkard father left us when I was four, and I haven't heard from him since. I grew up poor, basically working at a young age to get us through poverty. I had scholarships all throughout my education, and I became successful in what they call corporate life. I was in Panama 2 weeks ago to attend a business conference, and instead of taking my return flight, I decided to take the leap and purchase a one-way ticket to Buenos Aires. Now, I am here telling my story to a stranger in a nice restaurant overlooking the village of Mar del Plata," Elena said.

"That story sounds like pages of a novel," Javier replied.

"Probably if you look at it that way. The kind of rags to riches story," Elena quickly replied.

"Is this something common in the Philippines?" Javier asked.

"This is a common story in the Philippines. Poverty is rampant in provinces including Manila. The extreme contradiction of status in life is evident as you observe Manila. Beside the tall buildings lie the slums. The rich get richer and the poor get poorer," Elena continued.

"So, you probably feel proud that you finished your education and got out from the slums?" Javier stared at her with curiosity.

"Education is a good ticket out of poverty if you know how to play wisely. Most of the people in our village end up marrying early because of lack of money for education, and they embrace poverty because they are used to it," Elena replied.

"Interesting story," Javier replied.

The waiter came to take their orders. Javier managed to order for her in Spanish.

"Why Mar del Plata? You could have chosen Buenos Aires for instance, or Chile, or Brazil, or another big, nice city in Latin America."

"I met an old American couple on the plane on the way to Panama. They were doing a world tour and they mentioned this place. I don't know, but when I was in Panama airport waiting for my flight staring at the departure screen, there was a voice whispering for me to come here. And so, I did."

"Did you ever feel fear in making such a bold decision?" Javier asked.

"At first yes. I had this uncomfortable feeling in my stomach, but when I arrived here and saw the beautiful sea, I was at peace. The sea truly represents the name of this place, Mar del Plata – sea of silver. I met an old man giving me wisdom and guiding me on this little adventure. I am starting to enjoy it here and embrace the Argentinian way of life. It feels like home. Strange but true," Elena said.

"I am happy to hear that our small village feels like home

to you."

"How about you? What's your story?" Elena asked.

Before Javier could begin, the waiter arrived with their food. By the smell and the look, she knew it would be delicious.

"Well, I guess it's time to eat while the food is warm." Javier said with a smile.

Elena was thinking if this guy does not stop smiling, she would just melt where she was seated. His every smile and his gaze communicated with her on a deeper level.

They finished their meal satisfied and ordered a coffee to finish it off.

"You haven't told me your story," Elena said while they were waiting for their coffee.

"How about you meet me at Monumento al Lobo Marina tomorrow late in the afternoon, and I will tell you my story," Javier answered.

"You have the ability to provide suspense and excitement I would say. But yes, I would love to see that place," Elena answered.

"Good. I will see you tomorrow at 4 o'clock in front of the monument."

They finished their coffee and parted ways. Javier offered her a ride, but Elena decided to take the bus. She would love to be with this gorgeous guy for a little longer, but she decided to just take the bus. She remembered what Santiago told her during their first meeting – the art of patience.

10 THE EUPHORIA OF FIRST LOVE

Elena woke up full of energy and excitement. She would meet Santiago during noon for her usual lesson, and then she would meet Javier in the afternoon. It was unimaginable, the series of luck and changes that fate had led her to as soon as she took the risk of leaving her comfort zone. Accidental meetings with random strangers triggering bold steps and at the same time guiding her along the way.

She saw Santiago waving with a smile. As usual, he had gotten there early and was reading his book while he waited for her. He immediately stood up as she reached his table. He gave the usual beso. A few minutes later their coffee arrived. Perfect timing. The waiter already knew their order, and it arrived as soon as Elena arrived in the café.

"Come estas mi, bella dama?" Santiago asked.

"I am pretty well. I am enjoying my simple life here and starting to embrace the Argentinian way of living," Elena replied with a smile.

"Very well then! Did you finish your assignment for today?"

"I did!" Elena replied.

"Tell me, what do you want to become or to do after this little adventure of yours?"

"I achieved wisdom just by getting out of my comfort zone. I realized that the life I embrace in Manila is nothing but superficial. But I cannot blame anybody. It's culture and it's a product of the digital age and modernization,"

Elena replied.

"I have no doubt that you will come to this realization," Santiago affirmed his confidence with Elena.

Elena continued. "The ignorance lies in not being curious of other cultures, holding onto the typical standard accepted in my environment, and not exploring what is out there in the unknown. If only I knew I would have freedom as soon as I let go of all my fears, I would have done this a long time ago".

"Why haven't you done it long time ago?" Santiago knows how to trigger her buttons

"I believe that there is a timing for everything. I reached a level of unsatisfaction and emptiness which I should not see as bad, but a trigger to change. The perspective I lived and the experience is nothing but a simple bubble of comfort. I feel enlightened, and I want to share this experience and use it as a tool to educate people in Manila living a superficial life,"

"What will you do to share this enlightenment?" Santiago asked.

"When I go back to Manila, I will create a travel agency, but not a typical travel agency, to promote tourism. It will be a travel agency to promote cultural awareness and educate the young generation of Filipinos.

"Is Mar del Plata included in your travel destination?" Santiago never stopped.

"For sure. A lot of young professionals in the Philippines travel to our neighboring Asian countries and some travel to Europe or USA for the purpose of pleasure. That is okay because that's the purpose of travel, but I want to open horizons and encourage people to understand culture and local customs when traveling," Elena continued.

"Do you think you will be able to convince people with your new advocacy?" Santiago challenged.

"I know at first it would be difficult, but we should use travel as an opportunity to learn, to grow, and to understand different ways of living," Elena replied.

"You are becoming wiser than I am." finally Santiago agreed and laughed.

"You instilled in me a pearl of wisdom that I am grateful for. You taught me to understand life at its core and not by the surface. You made me realize so many things about my life, and through that, I know myself better," Elena immediately replied

"Is there no man involved in your plans?" Santiago teasingly asked.

"Santiago, you never fail to tease me!" A spark lit in Elena's eyes evident enough that it couldn't get past Santiago's scrutinizing gaze.

"I have a feeling you met a man. You don't have to say it, but I can see the glimmer in your eyes as soon as I asked the question." Santiago smiled.

"Well, I kept bumping into this stranger. I first saw in the little bookstore where I bought my journal. Yesterday, I met him in Torre del Monje, and he invited me to have lunch with him. I am meeting him this afternoon in Torre del Monje."

"Accidental meetings that could lead to a potential story. Enjoy the moment and do not rush. Destiny is written and should not be forced. Your trip here to Mar del Plata is not accidental at all, even if you think it was. You were guided along the way to find your purpose. I hope to meet this man making your eyes glimmer one day," Santiago replied.

"It's too early to tell, but I will absolutely tell you if things develop," Elena replied.

"I will wait for it," Santiago replied.

"How about you? You rarely talk about your life. I know your wife passed away two years ago and your son is depressed because his fiancée left him 6 months ago."

"I am seeing progress in him. I can see life coming back into his senses. I will give it time. Once I see he's all well and back to his normal routine, I will invite you to our humble abode for a little dinner."

"I will wait for it." Elena smiled.

They chatted and exchanged philosophical views until it was time for Elena to leave to meet Javier.

She arrived at Monumento al Lobo Marina and saw Javier standing near the statue of a sea lion.

"Good afternoon, Elena."

"Good afternoon. It's nice to see you once again," Elena replied.

"My pleasure. Let's go for a walk and watch the sea lions."

This was Elena's first experience watching sea lions. They walked along the shoreline watching them go back and forth to the water. Elena was thrilled watching these unbelievable creatures, full of beauty and energy, enjoying the breath of fresh seawater. They decided to have a seat after walking for a kilometer along the shoreline.

"You still owe me the story of your life. I just shared mine yesterday," Elena mentioned.

Javier smiled. "I guess I will not find an excuse today to not to tell you my story."

"I will not force you if you don't want to. You mentioned yesterday that you would share your story today, so I asked. If you don't feel comfortable, don't force yourself." Elena smiled.

"I was born and raised here in Mar del Plata. My father is a great guy full of wisdom. My mother was beautiful with a great heart but unfortunately, she passed away a few years ago. It has always been my passion to cook since I was a child. My parents sent me to a culinary school in France to fulfill my passion for cooking".

"Did you stay in France after your studies?" Elena asked.

"No. After my studies, I came back to Mar del Plata to open my own restaurant with financial help from my father. In my restaurant, I met this beautiful lady whom I proposed to during our 6th year anniversary. But almost a year ago, she left Mar del Plata to pursue her dreams.

"It must be hard when she left. Did you continue the relationship?" Elena again asked.

"We tried to make it work long-distance, but eventually we

broke our engagement. I want to follow her, but my life is here in Mar del Plata. I still blame myself sometimes for why things did not work out, but I guess we are not meant for each other. I cannot forever live with this pain. I must move on and that is what I have been doing. That's the reason you see me in these touristic places where we bumped into each other. I am re-affirming the reason I stayed here in Mar del Plata, because this is where I belong. I have my restaurant business which I really love. I inherited a small business from my father, but I decided to have a good friend of mine run it. I just serve as a part of the board of directors. I cannot live in an office. I love the kitchen. I love putting my creation into a meal and making people happy and satisfied after they eat what I prepared."

"That's an interesting story. Do you think your ex-fiancée will come back?" Elena unconsciously asked.

"I don't think so. She loves the big city life, the fast life, the glamour, and the superficial life which is the opposite of what I want. I honestly don't know how we lasted almost 7 years. Now I realize it will never work out because we want different lives," Javier added with a sad eye.

Javier's story reminded her of the story of Santiago's son. What are the odds to have a similar story in the same city? *Probably just coincidence*, she thought.

"What is your specialty in your restaurant?" Elena changed the subject.

"We cater traditional Argentinian food and contemporary French cooking. I want to serve traditional Argentinian food to tourists, and at the same time give a taste of French cuisine to locals. I want to share my experience in France through cooking," Javier replied.

"Can I try your restaurant one day?"

"Absolutely. You can come tomorrow for lunch then we can go to Plaza Colon for a walk," Javier replied.

"That sounds like a good plan. Alright, lunch tomorrow indeed. Would you mind if I show up at two in the afternoon? I need to meet my "guru" at noon."

"That would be perfect, as I will be busy from noon to around 2. By the time you arrive, the restaurant will be less busy, and we can enjoy a meal together. Give me your number and I will text you the address tomorrow morning," Javier replied.

"Well, you could give me the address now."

"You are killing the pleasure of suspense. I prefer to send you the address tomorrow." Javier smiled.

"Okay." *The art of patience*, Santiago's voice echoed in Elena's head.

They walked back to the statue of the sea lion. Javier insisted that he give her a ride back home, and Elena did not protest. They joked and laughed during the ride. At random, they discussed deep philosophical topics and then laughed again. They reached her apartment and Elena bid Javier goodbye.

She was in wonderland as she entered her apartment. She felt like a teenager wanting to jump, but at the same time, wanting to behave as an adult. There were butterflies in her stomach. It was the first time a man had given her butterflies in her stomach. She tried to calm down and told herself to relax and go with the flow. *Elena remember your stay here is not forever,* she told herself. *You will have to leave in three months. Let fate lead the way to what's in store.*

11 A LUNCH TO REMEMBER

Elena woke up and started her morning routine then off to meet Santiago. She hadn't received a text message yet from Javier with his restaurant's address. She tried to kill her overwhelming excitement. It was still early.

She met Santiago in their usual café. Since she didn't have an assignment from him, she guessed they would probably have a nice chat and exchange views and experiences.

She was happy she met Santiago. She realized that the sense of emptiness she somewhat felt was the longing for a father who could share her wisdom. Santiago filled that longing for a father figure she never had. Even if she never saw her father again, she was happy with her life and what she had become.

"I see that sparkle in your eyes glowing more and more each day. I smell a love story in the making," Santiago teased.

Elena laughed. "I found a father figure in you which I never had. I lost my fear for rejection."

"Beautiful. So, when do I meet this gorgeous stranger then?" Santiago didn't stop teasing.

"Someday soon I hope, Santiago. I just met him, and I am going with the flow. My stay in Mar del Plata is temporary. I still have a life to face and go back to," Elena replied.

"Is that what you want? To go back to your old life?" Santiago asked.

"No. I will never go back to my old life. I will live a

different life after this, but I have to wrap up my old life to have a complete peace of mind. My gorgeous stranger just came out of a long relationship. I don't want to jump into a relationship with him immediately. I don't want to find myself serving as a rebound," Elena replied.

"How long has your gorgeous guy been out of his previous relationship?" Santiago asked.

"He said almost a year," Elena replied.

"If you're not restricted with your stay in Mar del Plata, would you have a relationship with this guy?" Santiago never stopped asking questions

"Ah Santiago, you really know how to tease me. Honestly, I don't know."

"Just answer my question," Santiago insisted.

"Yes," Elena replied with doubt in her voice.

"Give it time. There is a reason why you landed here. Your accidental meetings are not accidental at all, it was bound to happen. There are no coincidences only synchronicities."

"Oh my God, you are saying the same things as this old couple I met on the plane," Elena replied.

"Because it's the truth. Soon you will be able to connect the dots out of this mystery. That is the beauty of embracing the unknown and trusting the rhythm of the universe. Every step is a learning process and once you fully learn the lesson, the gift of life will come."

"I will have to leave early today. I'm meeting my beautiful

stranger for lunch," Elena said smiling.

"Of course, mi bella dama. Go for it and savor the gift of getting to know a person. It's the most exciting part of a love story." Santiago smiled.

They were deep in conversation when Elena finally received a text message from Javier indicating the name and address of his restaurant. Elena bid Santiago goodbye.

The restaurant was a bit large and could accommodate around 60 people. It had a modest Argentinian ambiance and a European vibe. She went inside and saw Javier waiting for her with a smile. He led her to a table at the very corner of the restaurant, and soon a waiter served a good white Argentinian wine and empanadas.

Javier motioned to Elena to start eating the empanadas. He waited for her reaction after the first bite.

"This is so delicious. Better than any empanadas I tasted here in Mar del Plata," Elena exclaimed.

"Thank you. I prepared it myself," Javier replied.

"I cannot wait to see what you have for me for the main course."
"You have to wait and see, young lady. Get ready for the best meal of your life," Javier replied.

Elena stared at Javier as she finished chewing her third bite of empanada. "Are you always this calm and peaceful?"

"In general, yes, but for a long period of time, I was uneasy and restless. It's strange, but your presence somehow gave me some tranquility," Javier replied as he grabbed another empanada.

"Happy to hear that. Are you scared?" Elena continued.

"Scared of what?" Javier asked.

"Scared of getting into a relationship again." Elena stared directly into Javier's eyes.

"I don't know, only time will tell." Javier dismissed the conversation and avoided Elena's stare.

They finished the empanadas in between sipping wine, chatting and laughing. Elena was very happy, and she could say Javier was vibrating happiness, too. Their main course of locro arrived.

"I cooked this for you," Javier said.

"Oh, thank you."

"Go ahead," Javier said.

"Wow this is way better than the one I had in Torre del Monje," Elena said.

"Thank you," Javier replied with a smile.

They enjoyed the meal and finished it off with coffee. Javier stood up and told Elena he needed to go to the kitchen and would be back immediately.

When Javier came back a few minutes later, he told Elena it was time to go to Plaza Colon. Elena stood up and bid goodbye to the nice waiters who served them. Javier spoke to the waiters and headed towards Plaza Colon.

Plaza Colon is one of the most important green spaces in

Mar del Plata, mainly because of its privileged location, facing the casino and the sea. It was the place where the city's first cycling track was originally located. It had several statues such as that of Don Patricio Peralta Ramos - cast in bronze; the monument to Christopher Columbus - in marble, and the monument to Isabel La Católica amongst others.

They walked in the Plaza Colon laughing, chatting and again laughing. They looked like a happy couple. After more than an hour of walking, Javier told her he must go back to the restaurant to prepare for an important dinner service. Elena nodded and thanked Javier for the nice meal and walk.

Javier reached closely to her. She froze as she waited for what Javier would do. Javier gave her a kiss on the forehead, said thank you, and left. Elena was left in awe; she couldn't comprehend what just happened. They had a good time, but he only gave her a kiss on the forehead. She wanted more than that, but then again, a kiss on the forehead meant a lot especially coming from a Latino like him. It was a sign of respect and appreciation. After a few minutes, Elena caught her breath and walked towards the bus station towards home.

On her way to the bus station, her phone rang. It was Christina. It was expensive to take the international call, but she wanted to talk to her.

"Hello Christina, I missed you," she answered as she continued walking.

"Well my dear, you disappeared. Are you too busy at work? You haven't called me for a long period of time," Christina asked.

"Actually Christina, I am in Mar del Plata in Argentina, I did not go back home after my business trip."

"What?!

"Yes, sorry I did not tell you," Elena continued.

"I suggested you to take few days off but I did not expect you to take a long vacation. How about the job that you worked hard for, for sure this will have consequences? What if they fire you? Are you safe there?" Christina in her always blunt tone.

"I know. It's a long story. I have to go Christina; this would be an expensive call, but I promise I will call you some other time to explain and catch up," Elena apologetically continued. She saw the bus coming and she needed to end the call. Besides, she did not want to hear Christina's reality check.

"Ok, take care. Hopefully, your adventure is worth it. You just jeopardized your position and everything you worked hard for."

"I know. Really, I have to go now. Bye, thanks for the call and kiss Zach for me." She hanged up

She went up the bus and took a seat. On the road, her somewhat joyful state with Javier was replaced by thoughts about the phone conversation she had with Christina. She had not called Christina to inform her that she went to Mar del Plata. A few minutes ago, she was in ecstasy, now she was in torment being haunted by the life she left behind. She had come to the realization that she did not want to go back to her job anymore, but for a moment when Christina asked questions, she felt fear and doubt.

■ ■

Days and weeks passed, and it had become a routine for Elena to meet Santiago during noon and sometimes spend lunch with him. She also met Javier regularly. She didn't know what their relationship was, but she wasn't interested in labels. Her stay in Mar del Plata was temporary. In her heart, she didn't want to go back, but she had responsibilities and expectations. She would go with the flow and trust the universe for what it was about to bring.

She was meeting Javier for lunch in his restaurant. As usual, she was excited to see him. She entered the restaurant but did not see him. The waiters who knew her seated her at their usual table. After a few minutes, Javier came with a smile and his typical beso.

Minutes later the waiter came with their meal. They laughed and ate, not minding the time. Javier invited her to go to Torre del Monje again after checking the time. It was almost 5 o'clock. Elena couldn't believe time passed by so quickly.

It was almost 6 o'clock when they arrived in Torre del Monje. They went straight to the café-restaurant and Javier ordered two glasses of wine.

"Let's sit here and wait for the sunset," Javier said. They made themselves comfortable. "Tell me, how's your life like in Manila?"

"Nothing special I believe. I work hard but I also know how to enjoy life from time to time." Elena smiled. "I go out every Friday with my colleagues."

"What does go out mean?" Javier asked.

Elena hesitated to answer Javier's question but she

preferred to be honest. "We eat in fancy restaurants and go partying and clubbing afterwards."

"Party animal, huh?" Javier teased.

"Not really, it was a way for me to stop thinking about work for a moment and forget my responsibilities," Elena replied

"Does this partying bring you pleasure?" Javier asked as he signaled to one of his waiters for the bill

"Once in a while but in general, honestly no," Elena replied as she followed and tried to understand the hand signals of Javier to the waiter.

"Is somebody waiting for you back there?" Javier continued.

Elena started to feel uncomfortable with Javier's questions. At the same time, she felt that Javier wanted to get to know her deeper. "I wouldn't be here sitting with you if there was somebody waiting for me back home."

"So how come a beautiful woman like you is still single?" Javier never stopped.

Elena blushed. Javier's persistence reminded her of Santiago. "I honestly don't know. I always meet the wrong guys. I never really had a deep relationship. Besides, I never really had time for a relationship, I was too busy working."

"Congratulations," Javier said.

"What? Why? What do you mean," Elena replied confused. She didn't understand why Javier was congratulating her.

"You just found the right guy," Javier replied laughing with his index finger pointed to himself.

Elena laughed as well instead of responding.

"But I don't want to make promises," Javier continued in a flat tone.

They chatted and laughed as they enjoyed their wine.
Elena couldn't express the overwhelming happiness being in Javier's presence. When sunset came, Javier asked her to go to the edge of the restaurant to have a full view. Once they reached the view deck, Javier reached for her hand and his other hand reached her face. Before Elena knew it, a kiss landed on her lips. She closed her eyes and enjoyed the magical moment with Javier.

"I am thankful I met you. You gave me back my passion for life which I think I lost at some point. I enjoy talking to you and I love spending time with you. I am not sure where this is headed but there is something inside telling me it's okay and everything will be alright," Javier said after he kissed her
"There is something uncertain about the situation, but I feel the same. There is something inside me saying that everything is right," Elena replied.

They both knew there was uncertainty on what was about to come. It was not a secret that Elena's stay in Mar del Plata was temporary.

"Let me enjoy this moment while it lasts," Javier whispered to Elena.
"Me too, I hope for a miracle," Elena whispered back.
"I am scared to fall in love and get hurt again but I don't

want to think for now, let me live," Javier replied in his dry voice.

Elena decided not to say anything, she did not want to spoil the moment. Javier was scared to fall in love and get hurt again. She did not want to hurt him as well, but she did not want to stop either at this point. She felt that life was teasing her. She found somebody whom she could connect with and wished that this encounter could go deeper, but her current situation was uncertain.

He dropped her off at home. Before she could reach for the car door, Javier once again gave her a kiss.

"Have a good evening, mi bella dama," Javier said.

"Have a good evening too," Elena replied. Javier sounded like Santiago when he called her mi bella dama.

12 THE BIG REVELATION

Elena prepared herself for dinner at Santiago's house. She remembered Santiago telling her that his son was no longer depressed, and as a simple celebration, Santiago asked him to cook for his special guest.

Elena decided to wear a simple dress and just a bit of lipstick to add color to her makeup-free look. She was never fond of makeup anyway.
She rang the doorbell, and Santiago greeted her with a beso, full of smiles.

"Mi bella dama, welcome to my home. Come, and I will give you a tour of my humble abode while my son prepares our dinner," Santiago said.

Santiago motioned her to the living room with a traditional Argentinian vibe, but with minimal displays. A portrait of a young man and a woman hung on the wall. Santiago told her it was him and his wife a long time ago. The living room had two large, long sofas and two small sofas with white covers. There was a glass table at the center and an LED television in front. Though not the picture of luxury, it had a homey vibe to it.

Santiago also showed the patio, covered by well-maintained grass. Different flowers adorned the wall. There were a large barbeque place and a table with six chairs. It was a perfect patio for breakfast and dinners.

Finally, they reached the dining area. She could smell the food being prepared. She sat at the dining table, which was fully prepared with glasses and plates, restaurant-style. Then came a guy in an apron, a face and build so familiar to Elena that she just stared with wide eyes. Santiago's son stared at her with the same expression.

"From the way you stare at each other, it seems to me that you know each other," Santiago broke the silence in the awkward atmosphere.

"He's the one—" "She's the one—," they spoke at the same time then stopped.

"Alright kids, I need an explanation here. You first, my son." Santiago looked at Javier.

"She is the woman that I told you I met," Javier said.

"Connecting the dots, now I understand why Javier's mannerisms and personality are sometimes similar to yours. But you don't look like each other. Judging from the photo of your wife, now I understand that Javier got most of his features from her," Elena said staring at Santiago.

"Basically, my son is dating you, Elena?" Santiago asked.

"Elena is the woman you've been speaking about?" Javier asked his father.

"But I thought your son's name was Alex?" Elena asked staring at Santiago.

There was chaos in the conversation as everybody wanted to ask questions.

"Yes, she is the young woman I've been meeting and telling you about. The problem, son, is you tried to distance yourself, and I miss the company. I met this beautiful young lady, and she reminded me of your mother during our young days. I wanted to introduce her to you, but I tried to wait for the right time," Santiago explained.

"My name is Javier Alejandro. My father calls me Alex, short for Alejandro," Javier added.

"Santiago is this the son who you said was dumped by his fiancée a year ago?" Elena asked.

"Yes, he's my son I've been talking about. Little did I know, your gorgeous stranger is actually my son." Santiago started to laugh and clap. "Beautiful, beautiful," he added.

Javier and Elena stared at each other. They started to laugh as well.

They shared a great meal full of laughter. Life is so full of surprises sometimes and so hard to comprehend for Elena. There she was, having dinner with Santiago whom she loved dearly as a father, and with Javier the guy bringing her excitement every day, who happened to be Santiago's son. Elena couldn't comprehend all of life's surprises unfolding at the same time. It was too much of a coincidence for her. It felt unrealistic.

Santiago raised his glass of wine "I am happy that you're back and I can see life in you again," Santiago said, looking at Javier. "I hope you will continue like this. There are uncertainties and you probably have doubts, but let's trust and let go."

They ate and chatted in between, and laughter filled the dining table.

"I had a good meal with you kids. We should do this often, especially now that I learned that my son Javier is dating my lovely student Elena," Santiago remarked as they finish their meal.

"I would be happy to come over here for dinner," Elena

replied.

"And I would be happy to cook for two of my favorite people in the world," Javier replied.

They chatted more, laughed more, and drank more wine. Javier volunteered to take Elena back to her apartment. Silence ruled over in the car for a few minutes. Elena and Javier both tried to hold back their smiles.

"I cannot believe that the young lady my father is mentoring is actually you, Elena. And I cannot believe that the old man you're talking about is my father. I am happy you took that one-way trip to Buenos Aires and took that bus all the way to Mar del Plata.

"So, do you believe in destiny?" Elena asked Javier staring at the road.

"I do believe it's destiny. And thank you for giving company and bringing happiness to my father. I know I've been aloof at times, but I needed to mend my pain alone. But it's all good now. I am really happy." Javier broke the silence and reached for Elena's hand.

"I am happy too. Now that I try to connect the dots on how I met that old American couple, and how I landed in that small café and met your father. It was all synchronistic events. I found a father figure in your father. I felt a certain emptiness in my life, and when I met your father, I realized that this emptiness was caused by longing for the father I never had. Your father is full of wisdom, and he bestowed a lot of wisdom upon me. I am looking forward to seeing him every day," Elena replied.

"I know. I appreciate and love my father too much." Javier responded.

She was so happy but at the same time she was scared. This was just too good to be true, and it would bring her too much pain if she left this state. *Enjoy the moment*, a voice in her head echoed.

They both stared at each other and Javier planted a simple kiss on Elena's lips. When they reached Elena's apartment, Javier got out of the car and opened Elena's door. He reached for her hand, touched her face, and kissed her passionately. That night, they fully expressed their feelings for each other, bathing in each other's arms the entire night.

"Come to our house tomorrow evening for another dinner. Papa will be happy to have you for company," Javier said.

"With pleasure," Elena replied.

■■■

Days and weeks passed by, and it had become a normal routine for Elena to meet Javier every other day and Santiago on alternate days. She had become a regular guest in their house for dinner. They also started having regular Sunday lunch in Santiago's garden.

Happiness, contentment, and blessings were beyond expression for Elena. The risk and embracement of the unknown to find the answer for the longing in her soul led her to greatness. She now started to believe in destiny. She started to understand why she was never successful with men in the Philippines. She realized that the story was already written; all the experiences she had in life were necessary for her to be able to appreciate what was to come. She hated her upbringing from poverty, but it taught her to work hard and crave success. The superficial life she got used to, made her appreciate simple things. The idea of following society's standard pushed her to defy the norm and follow her heart. All the contradictory and difficult experiences she never understood why she had to undergo were purely an appetizer for the main course in life. She realized that happiness started from within. When she started to find herself, she found a teacher of life, and when she learned the lessons in life, she found love.

Before going to bed, Elena prayed like she never prayed before, but not to ask for something, but purely to thank God for the destiny that was written for her. She slept with a smile and looked forward to the next day.

The end to Elena's three-month stay in Argentina was fast approaching. Her visa was valid for one year with multiple entry, but she was limited to a 90 day stay, and that ended in two weeks. She originally intended to visit either Brazil or Argentina, which was the reason she applied for both visas before her business trip. She was happy she went to Mar del Plata on impulse and braved taking off three months.

She told herself better to have both just in case. She was thinking the expensive visa application fees and the expedite processing fees that she paid were worth it. Although she still couldn't comprehend why citizens of third world countries have to pay for an expensive visa, while citizens of first world countries could enter without a visa. Life was unfair sometimes; the poor get punished while the rich get free tickets. But well, that was not part of her concern now. She didn't want to end this fairy tale, but there were restrictions and she also had responsibilities. She believed the time would come for her and Javier to be together, but for now she needed to provide closure to her previous life. She loved and respected the people she worked with, both her team and her bosses. This village called sea of silver had given her treasure, but she knew that in order to fully embrace this new beginning, she needed closure in her previous life. Although she was scared that once she returned to the Philippines, she might never come back to Argentina.

She didn't have the courage to tell Santiago and Javier that she only had two weeks' valid stay in Argentina. It would break her heart and theirs.

13 THE PAINFUL DEPARTURE

Elena had only three days left before the validity of her stay expired. Overstaying would make her an illegal alien in Argentina. That wasn't an option since being forced to leave by officials meant she would never be able to return to Argentina. There was only one choice left: she needed to go back to Philippines to sort out the life she left. Her situation in Mar del Plata was too good to be true, and she was afraid that at some point it would be taken away from her. She needed to get out of this unbelievable bliss for a moment to provide closure to her previous life and think about how to proceed next.

She sighed and inhaled deeply; she would purchase a one-way ticket to go back to the Philippines.

She clicked the "confirm" button. Ticket purchased, time to go back to reality.

Since she did not have the courage to tell Santiago or Javier that she would be leaving in three days, she decided to write a letter for both of them.

My Dearest Santiago,

I cannot be thankful enough to God that he led me to you. All these years that I was wondering what I was missing in my life, I was actually missing the father figure I never had. I was blessed enough to experience that moment with you, even just for a short period of time. When I was young, I thought I was punished by God because I never grew up with my father. Now I realize I had to undergo all these circumstances because it would make me strong and teach me a significant lesson in life. I found myself, I found you, and I found Javier. Even if it's just temporary, I am grateful for all the moments and lessons we shared.

I have to leave Argentina and go back to the Philippines. I need to sort out my reality in order for me to take the right direction. I will not say goodbye, who knows what's out there.

Elena

She finished the letter with a heavy heart. She put it in an envelope and wrote Santiago's home address. She started on the hard part, the letter to Javier.

Javier,

I am sorry. I cannot say this in person because it would break my heart and I know it will break yours as well, but I have to leave Argentina and go back to the Philippines. It is a painful decision, but I have to respect regulations. I also have to sort out my reality in order to move on and take the right direction.

No words can express how happy I am with the short period of time we shared. I am thankful to God that I met you, you gave me hope and love. I don't know what is out there, but I do believe that if it's meant to happen, it will. I will follow the flow of the universe and if that flow brings me back to you, it would be the happiest day of my life. If not, then I am still happy because the moments I shared with you are indescribable. I hope to see you again. Hugs and kisses.

Elena

Tears flowed as she finished the letter. She put it in an envelope and addressed it to Javier's restaurant.

She would send the letters on her last day in Mar del Plata. For now, she needed to meet Santiago and Javier for lunch at their house. Their Sunday lunch had become a tradition.

She rang the doorbell. Javier, smiling, opened the door. They kissed as she entered the house. They went straight to the patio where a table was set with plates and glasses. It was a beautiful day. It was a good day to celebrate their great life together, a gift so precious that no amount of money could buy.

"Elena, it feels like you've been with us for a long period of time. How long have you been here now in Mar del Plata?" Santiago asked.

"Indeed. It feels so natural and serene that I lost count of the days I've been here." Elena avoided answering the question.

"So, what are your plans now?" Santiago asked.

"That's a good question Santiago. I thought about that this morning. Maybe it's time for me to think about how I can find a job here in Mar del Plata," Elena replied again, trying to hide the truth about her departure.

"Well, you can help me and my father run our small business. You're a businesswoman, so you would do well." Javier joined the conversation.

"Oh, thank you, that's really a great offer. Give me a few days to think about it," Elena replied.

"Well then, should we have a toast for a new partnership?" Santiago raised his glass. They all raised their glasses while Elena cried inside.
Tomorrow she would mail the letters before she took the

bus to Buenos Aires. She would spend one night in Buenos Aires before taking her flight back to Manila. This was her last day with them.

"So, what are your plans tomorrow?" Javier asked Elena.

"Uhm, I need to take care of some administrative stuff tomorrow for my stay in Argentina. I am afraid it will consume my entire day, so I will not be available. However, I would like to invite you back to my apartment tonight," Elena said with a wink. She tried to control her emotions as much as possible.

"Do I need to reserve a lot of energy for tonight?" Javier asked with a naughty smile.

"I guess so. The more energy the better," Elena replied.

They laughed.

That night, Elena savored every minute of her last moment with Javier. In the afternoon the next day, she took the bus to Buenos Aires for her flight back to the Philippines.

14 GOING BACK TO REALITY

"Passengers of Flight LA458 bound to Santiago, the boarding gate is open."

Elena sighed. Aside from the fact that she left with a heavy heart, this would be a long flight. She booked a cheap ticket with three layovers: Buenos Aires to Santiago, Chile; Auckland, New Zealand; and Sydney Australia. She and Javier literally lived on opposite ends of the world.

She had the option for one or two layovers, but it was too expensive. Before, she didn't agree that money could buy time, but now she realized that the sentiment was true. She needed to pay for an expensive ticket to have a shorter flight. A business class ticket would allow her to skip long security and boarding lines. She needed to pay expedited services in order to have priority processing for visas. Even the worst traffic in Manila could be beaten by a helicopter if you have the money. Having money could give you the means to speed things up in life. It was a sad but true reality.

She fastened her seatbelt as the seatbelt sign lit up. She was now in Sydney, the last connection before she landed in Manila. She watched six movies and barely slept. She was so tired, and all she wanted now was a good shower and the comfort of her bed.

So many thoughts lingered in her head. Her experience in the last three months played in her thoughts like scenes in a movie. It felt unreal, but at the same time, it felt so real that it made going back seems like the worst decision to make. But let bygones be bygones. She would start a new life.

She opened her door and was welcomed by the familiarity

of her apartment. She couldn't ignore the awkward feeling deep inside that she no longer belonged here. She loved this apartment, she always dreamed of having one like this, but now she felt the opposite. She dropped her luggage, went straight to shower, and tucked herself in bed and slept.

■■

Time to face the moment of truth. She looked at the tall building; the day had come for her to face the reality that she avoided for three months. Her resignation letter was officially signed and ready to be handed over to her boss. She inhaled deeply and entered the building.

"Honestly, I am really disappointed with your decision," her boss said calmly. "You are one of the best, and I always thought you had a big career ahead of you. I was actually thinking of you as my replacement when I retire."

"I am really sorry for all the inconvenience I caused." Elena stared apologetically at her boss.

"I don't know what else to say. You broke my trust and defied my expectations," her boss continued.

She expected the discussion to be calm, but it was the opposite. She was also disappointed with herself, but there was no sign of regret. In the end, her boss forgave her for the fiasco and betrayal she committed. She gave her blessing and wished her good luck. There was no point for Elena to continue on in her job. She lost their trust by taking that one-way ticket to Buenos Aires and being AWOL for three months. She was not sure what to do next, but for now she needed to wrap up her business affairs.

She went to see her team. They were all happy to see her

back, but at the same time saddened by the news that she was leaving the company.

"You owe me a story, boss," Tina demanded.

"There is no story to tell Tina. But if there is one thing I can share with you—I found myself and peace," she replied, her voice saying the opposite.

She tried to make the meeting brief, as she didn't want to share any details or a story.

She went back home to see her mother and told her the story of her life in the last three months. Her mother asked her about her plans, and all she could manage to answer was, "I'm not sure for now."

She went to see Christina and finally told her the entire story. She remembered their phone conversation when she was in Mar del Plata. Christina was concerned with her decision but hearing the entire story, Christina was so happy and applauded Elena for the guts.

"I will not give you any advice because I know you will find clarity and your own answers. Whatever your decision, I will support you." Christina said.

"Thank you, Christina."

■■■

More than a month had passed since she left Mar del Plata, and not a day went by when she didn't think of Santiago and Javier. She needed to get out of the bustling life of Manila in order to be able to think clearly. She went to the beach to clear her head and to work on her business plan to open a travel agency.

She woke up one day feeling dizzy and unwell. She felt the overwhelming urge to vomit. She had a healthy meal, so there was no way that her upset stomach could be caused by anything she ate yesterday. It suddenly dawned on her that she hadn't had her period for one month now. Could it be a possibility that she was pregnant? She was nervous and started to sweat. She went to the pharmacy to buy a pregnancy test.

She followed the instructions on the pregnancy kit. She was so nervous that she didn't want to see the result. *What would I do if I am pregnant? I was so stupid not to use any protection,* she thought. *But on the other hand, it's about time for me to get pregnant. I'm not getting any younger. Besides, I will have a cute child.*

"Ugh, I need to stop thinking. I will die of stress!" Elena shouted.

Finally, the pregnancy test revealed the results. Positive. She could not believe it. She wanted to see a doctor to double check. She was nervous, but at the same time happy. It was a gift. She and Javier had created life.

After her visit to the doctor, it was confirmed. She was pregnant. Her life was getting more complicated now that she was carrying a life inside her. She didn't know what to do. She went from being enlightened to being lost again.

■■

In Mar del Plata, Santiago and Javier were having a dinner.

"Did you hear anything from Elena?" Santiago asked looking at Javier's eyes.

"No" Javier shortly answered avoiding his father's stare.

"Why don't you call her?" Santiago continued.

"Papa, when I started seeing Elena, it was not something serious because I knew her stay was temporary. I enjoyed the moment with her for sure," Javier answered.

"Don't you miss her?" Santiago never stopped

"She was interesting, I enjoyed learning her culture, I enjoyed our conversation and the times we shared together but that's it." Javier replied in a flat tone.

"But don't you want to work it out?" Santiago insisted.

"She left without saying goodbye. I did not like the way she handled the situation. And, if possible, I don't want to talk about her anymore." Javier dismissed the conversation.

Santiago was left in silence and did not bother to ask questions. Javier was not showing emotion at all. At some point he, himself had doubts about the relationship but disregarded the thought. He knew that if it was meant to happen, it will.

He knew Elena very well. He knew that Elena did things for a reason and he was confident that Elena would get in touch with them at some point. He knew that Elena had to settle the responsibilities that she had left behind. *Give it time.*

15 FOLLOWING THE FLOW OF THE UNIVERSE

For few days, Elena tried to clear her head to determine what to do next. She was carrying Javier's child. She had left Mar del Plata without saying a proper goodbye, she had just left a letter. She didn't know if she would still be accepted by Javier after what she had done. But she knew that Javier deserved to know that she was carrying his child. Abortion was not an option for her, but she was also scared to raise a child without a father. She didn't want her child to grow up without a father and experience what she had. It would be unfair for her to deny her child a father.

She still had savings left but buying a ticket to Argentina would mean she would consume almost all her savings. If things didn't work out between her and Javier, she would have financial challenges.

"Ah so many what if's," Elena murmured.

At the end of the day, she made her decision. She would book a one-way ticket going back to Argentina. She would not know the answer unless she tried it first. If Javier rejected her then it was okay, she would figure out what to do next when she got there.

■ ■

A woman with a familiar figure was sitting at the reserved table. Elena. She sat there with a smile on her face but longing and fear in her eyes. She dried her sweaty palms on her jeans. Javier approached her, grabbed a chair and joined her.

"I am listening." Those are the only words he managed to say. He knew that Elena would leave Mar del Plata, but he was disappointed to receive a goodbye letter. He couldn't understand why Elena left without a proper goodbye.

"I don't know where to start, but first I am really sorry for not saying a proper goodbye. My 90 day stay here in Argentina had expired. I didn't want to overstay because that can lead to a forced departure and the possibility to be denied entry in Argentina again. I left unfinished business in Philippines that I needed to wrap up in order for me to move forward." Elena sighed. "I wanted to tell you the truth, but I didn't have the courage to say so. I am scared of your reaction and what will happen. I am here not only to ask your forgiveness but to tell you something."

"What is so difficult about telling the truth? I would understand if you told me the truth about your situation," Javier replied in a dry voice. "I knew it would be just temporary, it wasn't a secret that you had a visa restriction. Honestly, I was not expecting more in our relationship. I always kept in mind that it would only be temporary, but unfortunately I felt something different when you left." Javier stared at her. "I thought what we shared was real, but then maybe not because you left without saying anything. I found a letter two days after you left without any explanation," Javier continued.

"I know, and I'm sorry," Elena replied.

"I don't know if I can trust you. I don't want another heartbreak. It is too much for me to take. I feel that you would just leave me like that whenever you want. I have been left once. I will not allow any woman to do that to me again," Javier said in a firm tone.

"I absolutely understand Javier. If you don't want me in your life anymore, then I will respect that. I came here to ask for nothing except your forgiveness, and to tell you what you deserve to know. You deserve to know the truth." There was a pause for a moment. Elena inhaled deeply. "I am pregnant."

Javier was left blank and didn't know what to say. He stood up and left the table.

■■

"Papa can I ask you something?" Javier asked while having dinner with Santiago.

"What made you fight for your love with Mama?" Javier continued.

"I didn't have to ask myself, I just knew" Santiago replied. "Why? Are you still thinking of Elena?"

"She came to the restaurant today. She is back here in Mar del Plata. She asked for forgiveness. She didn't mention getting back together, but she told me that she is pregnant," Javier said in a casual tone.

"Mi hijo, forget about your pride and whatever grudge you feel in your heart. Elena is a good person. She left Mar del Plata for a good reason. She doesn't have to tell me, but I know she had a good reason. She didn't mention getting back together, but I know deep inside her that's what she wishes for. She was raised by a single mother. Coming to the opposite side of the world to see you means a lot. I know she doesn't want to deny her child a father. She is back here with the hopes that you will take her back," Santiago replied.

"But how do you know these things, Papa? You didn't talk to her. She didn't even say a proper goodbye, just a letter to both of us."

"I don't need explanations, I just know. So, if I were you, I would get up now and go back to her before it's too late,"

Santiago continued.

Javier was silent for a moment, trying to digest what his father said.

Yes, this was the second time a woman left him, but this time she came back. Not alone but with a life inside her womb, his child. He could have his pride, but is he willing to sacrifice his pride for his happiness? He had fallen in love with Elena. His father was probably right. He got up quickly.

"Send my regards to her and tell her she owes me a visit," Santiago said as Javier quickly moved towards the door. Santiago flashed a knowing smile as Javier bid him goodbye.

■■

There was a hard knock on the door. Elena was lying down in bed, her eyes swollen from crying. She was still tired from the long flight, but she couldn't sleep because of jet lag. The hard knock continued. Elena slowly moved towards the door. She was a bit annoyed that someone was visiting so late.

She opened the door and found Javier standing there with a bouquet of flowers that looked freshly picked from their garden. The flowers were held together with a knot.

"Can I come in?" Javier asked after a moment of silence.

Elena found her voice. "Yes, sure."

As soon as Elena closed the door, Javier grabbed and hugged her.

"I don't want to ever lose you again. This time no more

secrets. We will raise our child together," Javier said.

"And by the way, the flowers are for you. Sorry I didn't have the time to buy something nice," Javier continued.

Elena was still speechless. She put the flowers immediately on the sofa.

Javier tried to grab something inside his pocket. It was a small box. He kneeled and opened it.

"Will you marry me?" Javier asked.

Elena was still speechless. "I don't know what happened to you, but have you lost your tongue?" Javier said jokingly to lighten the mood.

"Is this your previous engagement ring?" Elena finally managed to speak.

Javier laughed. "Of all the words you could say, that's the first thing? Yes, it is the previous engagement ring. I didn't have time to buy a new one since your visit came by surprise," Javier said.

"Do you promise you will buy me a new one?" Elena insisted with a teasing smile.

"Oh God seriously, answer my question first before I answer your question," Javier laughed.

Elena laughed and cried at the same time. She hugged Javier. "Yes, mi amor."